Robert G. Barrett was raised in Sydney's Bondi, where he worked mainly as a butcher. He moved to Terrigal on the Central Coast of New South Wales, where after twenty-five years and much hard work he managed to forge a career as a successful writer.

Also by Robert G. Barrett
and published by HarperCollins:

HIGH NOON IN NIMBIN

ROBERT G. BARRETT

HarperCollinsPublishers

HarperCollins*Publishers*

First published in Australia in 2009
This edition published in 2010
by HarperCollins*Publishers* Australia Pty Limited
ABN 36 009 913 517
www.harpercollins.com.au

Copyright © Psycho Possum Productions Pty Ltd 2009

The right of Robert G. Barrett to be identified as the author of this
work has been asserted by him under the *Copyright Amendment
(Moral Rights) Act 2000*.

HarperCollins*Publishers*
Level 13, 201 Elizabeth Street, Sydney NSW 2000, Australia
Unit D, 63 Apollo Drive, Rosedale, Auckland 0632, New Zealand
A 53, Sector 57, Noida, UP, India
1 London Bridge Street, London SE1 9GF, United Kingdom
2 Bloor Street East, 20th floor, Toronto, Ontario M4W 1A8, Canada
195 Broadway NY, NY 10007, United States of America

National Library of Australia Cataloguing-in-Publication data:

Barrett, Robert G.
   High noon in Nimbin / Robert G. Barrett.
   ISBN: 978 0 7322 8758 0 (pbk.)
   Norton, Les (Fictitious character) – Fiction.
   Nimbin (N.S.W.) – Fiction.
A823.3

Cover design by Matt Stanton, adapted by Kerry Klinner, Megacity Design
Cover images: gun by Matt Stanton, all other images by Shutterstock.com
Author photo: Sarhn McArthur Photography
Typeset in 11/16pt Minion by Kirby Jones
Printed and bound in Australia by McPherson's Printing Group
50gsm Bulky News used by HarperCollins*Publishers* is a natural, recyclable
product made from wood grown in sustainable plantation forests. The
manufacturing processes conform to the environmental regulations in the
country of origin, New Zealand.

DEDICATION

I want to dedicate this book to two
footballers, Andrew Johns and
Wendell Sailor. Not because I'm a
rugby league nut or I'm a particular
fan of theirs, but these two men took
a bit of a fall and got hammered
unmercifully by the media only for
being who they are. Yet they took it on
the chin and bounced back bigger and
better than ever. I think this is full-on
Australian and highly admirable.
Onya boys.

A MESSAGE FROM THE AUTHOR

I imagine everybody's wondering why I'm late getting a book out this year. Well, I've had a few ups and downs and other things on my plate. I won't go into any great detail here. But everything is explained on my website along with a heap of photos from the waxhead wedding of the year and others taken in Nimbin. I've also posted a photo some diggers sent me from Iraq, of them aboard a new super-stealth helicopter the Australian government is ordering. It's highly classified and I'll no doubt get myself into all sorts of trouble for publishing this photo; either ASIO will assassinate me or the CIA will whisk me off to Guantanamo Bay. But these are just the things I do for my readers and I like to live dangerously. There's also photos of me wearing some kit I got sent from an adjutant librarian in Afghanistan in exchange for two boxes of my books. I look pretty cool.

Again I have to apologise to all the people who wrote to me and haven't got a reply yet. I do my best. But there's just so many letters and because of the ups and downs this year I haven't had a chance to reply to all of them. But now that the book's finished I'm slowly but surely ploughing through them and you should get a reply. However, if you miss out, don't worry. I read and appreciate every letter I get. And didn't I get some letters from my WA readers with ideas for a story set over there. Thank you to all the sand gropers. I'll do a Les Norton in WA one day for sure. I've got enough ammunition for ten books.

A lot of people send me manuscripts they've written hoping to get published. To be honest, there's not a great deal I can do except give them a quick read then pass them on to my editor. And so far she hasn't uncovered the next J.K. Rowling or Dan Brown. She hasn't even uncovered another Barbara. But don't give up. If you think you've got a half readable book in you, have a go.

There's a lot of different music in this book and I don't mean to come over as some kind of musical snob. But it's all good foot stompin, get-down rock 'n roll and, being a grumpy old man, I have to admit

I can't stand that doof-doof house music. It gives me carbuncles. All the CDs I bought mostly at JB HiFi at Erina Fair. They've got a great selection. I thoroughly recommend Lucy De Soto and the Phantom Blues Band. You'll have a hard time trying to find those two Doors albums they did after Jim Morrison died, but if you can they're well worth it. Ray Manzarek on piano is a pure genius.

I suppose I should apologise to two good friends of mine, Tony Nolan and Sean Doherty. These two blokes did me an immeasurable favour and I repaid them by stitching them up in this book. But what would you expect from a miserable old dropkick like me? And it was all done in the very best of taste.

To all those people wanting Team Norton T-shirts and caps, I've still got plenty. But some types are a bit thin on the ground. Plus my regular screenprinter has disappeared into the jungles of Vietnam with all the CD-roms. Rather than send an assassin after him in a patrol boat to terminate him with extreme prejudice, I've found another bloke. I got some more printed. But he's flat out setting everything up. So put your phone number in with your order and we can get back to you if we haven't got the T-shirt you want. Or you can put in another preference. I can also get books if you're having trouble finding them. Same price as the T-shirts and caps: $30.00 postage paid. And seeing I'm such a good bloke, I'll even autograph them for you. Unfortunately we can't do overseas orders.

Well, that's about it, folks. I hope you enjoy *High Noon in Nimbin*. It was a hard one to write and I'm sorry it was late arriving. But everything is explained on my website. Nevertheless, I think it turned out all right. Now all I have to do is try and write another one. Thanks for your support. You're the best.

Robert G. Barrett

HIGH NOON IN NIMBIN

It was a dirty, rotten, low-down thing to do. It was callous and it was mean. It was wanton and shameful and despicable bordering on repugnant. Besides that, the victim of this loathsome deed belonged to an endangered and protected species, making the insidious act an environmental atrocity. Certainly nothing to be proud of. And Norton knew it. However, instead of showing any remorse, pangs of conscience or a sense of shame for his part in the vile, reprehensible crime, the big redheaded Queenslander was grinning from ear to ear. Laughing. Singing, even. But what would you expect from a ruthless low-life thug working on a door in Kings Cross?

The whole unseemly incident revolved around a poor inoffensive little green tree frog that had set himself up somewhere around the fountain in Norton's backyard during the mating season. Les had never managed to lay eyes on the frog, but he nicknamed him Fabio. Happily ensconced at Chez Norton, Fabio used to spend the evenings sending out his sweet love song to any female frogs in the hood who might be interested in dropping by for a bit of conversation and company. Or to put it in the great Australian vernacular, Fabio was trying like mad to get himself a root.

Fabio would generally start serenading around nine in the evening, then go through non-stop till sunrise. Fabio's idea of a love song was to puff up a large membrane of flesh under his chin then explode it with a resonating 'PWOP' that could be heard a block away. He'd work Norton's backyard till midnight, then move down the side passage between Norton's bedroom and the house next door on the right that belonged to Norton's new and likeable architect neighbour Ross and his wife Polly.

Both Ross and Polly had a green thumb and together they'd put a flower-filled rockery in their bricked-off front yard along with a small fountain, gnomes and other things. A wrought iron fence with a couple of holes in the bottom separated the two houses and Fabio figured if he couldn't pull a sheila at Les's, he might find one next door. Entice her through the fence back to his bachelor pad at Chez Norton, throw some Barry White on the stereo, knock up a jug of margharitas and then toss her up in the air.

Unfortunately, female frogs were very thin on the ground in Bondi and despite his endless serenading, Fabio was having no luck with the ladies at either venue. Also unfortunately for Fabio, he could have chosen a better spot than Chez Norton to operate. Fabio and his serenading was now giving the owner a full-on, galloping case of the shits. A case of the shits that was getting worse all the time.

When Fabio was serenading in the backyard it wasn't so bad and only sounded like a faint 'pwop' in the distance. But when Fabio set himself up outside Norton's bedroom, it was no different to someone bursting a paper bag beneath the side window every ten seconds — ruining Norton's sleep, giving him bags under his eyes and driving the big Queenslander into a frenzy. And the noise seemed to get louder as the night wore on.

Les tried ear plugs. But they'd end up falling out and they made the insides of his ears itch. He went out with a baseball bat to smash Fabio's head in, pots of boiling water to scald him, and plastic containers of hydrochloric acid to burn him. But Fabio tap danced too fast in the darkness for Les and Norton couldn't even catch a glimpse of the green demon let alone get his hands on him. Because of the noise and the risk of ricocheting bullets, Les stopped himself from grabbing a gun and emptying a few clips in Fabio's direction. But he was seriously considering getting a stick of dynamite and concocting a story about unknowingly crossing a team of nutters in Kings Cross who wanted him dead; bad luck about the collateral damage to his bedroom and Ross and Polly's front yard. But Les had to do something. Fabio was turning Norton's life into a living hell and it was only a matter of time before he put Les in a straightjacket.

There was only one answer: Les had to organise a hit on Fabio. A contract killing. And although it was going to the ultimate extreme, calling in one of Sydney's deadliest hitmen to take out a frog, it had to be done. So on a cool Monday morning in Bondi, halfway through autumn, Norton picked up his land line and phoned Eddie Salita.

'Yeah hello.'

'Eddie. It's Les.'

'Hey, Les. How are you, mate?'

'Not bad. Hey, Eddie, did I leave my sunglasses in your car?'

Misplaced sunglasses was a code they used at the Kelly Club. It meant a deadly serious situation had arisen. Murder was in the air. Drop everything and get to the source ASAP.

There was a brief pause on the line. 'Yeah. I think you did,' replied Eddie. 'You home now?'

'Yes.'

'I'll see you in … twenty minutes.'

Les hung up and stared at the phone. 'Fabio,' he said, a sinister smile edging around his tired, darkened eyes, 'with a bit of luck, you are a dead frog hopping.'

Les got up, went to the kitchen and poured himself a glass of cold milk. Then, still wearing his old black trackies and daggy grey sweatshirt, returned to the loungeroom, sat down and ruminated on life while he waited for Eddie.

All in all, life was pretty good. When his face healed up, Les borrowed Billy's Holden station wagon and drove back to Terrigal, where he met Marla and had a delightful lunch at the Haven, promising to see her again as soon as things quietened down in the motel trade. Warren was back in Surfers Paradise shooting a TV commercial for some white-shoe developers, and although the boarder had stitched him up in the search for Bodene's film script, Les finally saw the funny side of it and decided against boiling Warren in rancid chicken fat; although the 1930 penny turning up out of the blue certainly sweetened things up a lot. Beatrice said it was worth at least $35,000. But outstanding rarities like that you just didn't sell. So Warren's girl got Les a certificate of verification, had the old coin insured and locked it in her safe for him. Leaving Les still wedged behind the eight ball in his search for a lazy fifty to dump his old Holden and buy the hybrid German car he fancied — unless he wanted to cut into his stash buried in the backyard. But Les would sort it out somehow. Of course there was always the odd glitch in life. In this case, like everybody else at the Kelly Club, Les was temporarily laid off.

A film company had approached Price to use the front of his club during the day for a crime series being shot in Sydney's Eastern Suburbs called *Gut Feeling*. Price liked the irony of it all and also liked the nice little earner the film company had offered him. Unfortunately, the stunt driver for an action scene was like the idiot on *The Fast Show*. He lost control of a flatbed Holden roaring down Kelly Street and ploughed straight into the front door of the club, smashing the foyer to pieces, breaking both his legs and setting the stairs on fire. Only for the quick arrival of the fire brigade, it was lucky the

Kelly Club and the buildings on either side didn't go up. While Les and the others were laughing fit to bust and pasting the newspaper clippings in their scrapbooks, Price blew a gasket before settling down and suing everybody concerned for damages, loss of income, post traumatic stress disorder and anything else he could think of. The end result was, Les and Billy would be back at work in a brand new foyer with new carpet and a better door, and Price would be around another million in front. When it came to turning shit into Chanel No. 5, nobody could get within a bull's roar of the dapper, silvery-haired casino owner.

Another glitch, if you could call it that, was that Les had received an invitation to a wedding between Steve 'Deadline' Deverell, the waxhead editor of a surfing magazine called *Off Shore*, and his girlfriend Ninety-Nine, two people Les had got to know through Tony Nathan, aka Steelo, the surf photographer. Steve had a deadly sense of humour behind a pair of mercurial dark brown eyes, and with his shaved head and square jaw, always reminded Les of Jason Statham from the Transporter movies. Steve got the nickname Deadline because he preferred surfing to work and was always on deadline. His girlfriend Saretta got the nickname Ninety-Nine because she looked a lot like Maxwell Smart's good-looking assistant, right down to the prominent cheekbones and shiny brown hair. They'd been together three years and had two lovely little daughters so Steve decided to tie the knot. The wedding was on Wednesday at Wallis Lake just north of the Myall Lakes near Forster on the New South Wales north coast. Go up Tuesday. Come back Thursday. And Les for the life of him didn't want to go. It wasn't the drive, or knowing Steve's waxhead mates would drive him crazy with their 'unreal tubes man' and 'ohh those waves were filthy man' or 'that last session was really sick man'. Or being billeted for two nights in a holiday apartment at Blueys Beach with snail's pace Tony Nathan. Les simply hated weddings. At all the ones he'd been to, the guests were generally married couples and Les, the perennial bachelor hanging around on his own, always felt like a Jew with a piano accordion at a Hitler Youth rally. However, Les couldn't get out of it because he pretty much owed Steve Deverell his life. More than that, Deadline saved Les the ignominy of having his big boofhead splashed all around Australia on prime-time TV.

Les had got into a massive drink one summer Sunday night at the Bondi Icebergs and woke up sick as a dog the next morning. He couldn't handle any breakfast, so he shuffled miserably down to South Bondi to have a swim and liven up a little, before pouring several strong coffees down his throat and a packet of Panadeine. As he dropped his T-shirt and towel on the sand, Les noticed the film crew from *Bondi Rescue* were positioned at the water's edge with the local lifeguards waiting for some stupid Jap or Eurotrash backpacker to get into difficulties so the lifeguards could paddle furiously out through the break and make a dramatic, action-packed, fully televised rescue. The surf was only moderate so, wearing an old pair of blue shorts, Les plunged in and began lazily swimming and drifting out through the waves and surfers.

The water was delightful and Les was starting to rejoin the land of the living when he found himself caught in a rip. It wasn't very strong and Les knew if he just went with it and swam to the side he'd eventually find himself on a sandbank. Les was casually breaststroking along when some bloated lilywhite backpacker on a hired mini-mal picked up a wave and fell off the moment he got to his feet. As he did, he kicked the mini-mal forward and it speared Norton in the ribs, forcing Les to clench his jaw and clutch at his side. The pain felt like when he was sparring with Billy Dunne and Billy would suddenly weave and hammer a left rip below Norton's floating rib into his liver, stopping the big Queenslander in his tracks. While the backpacker ignored Les and clambered back onto his surfboard, Les held his ribs, hardly able to breathe. Nothing appeared to be broken, but he'd definitely torn a rib cartilage and he was in trouble.

Just managing to tread water, Les drifted back into the rip where a couple of bigger waves broke over him, tossing him helplessly around in the foam. Another wave broke on him, keeping him under, and in his semi-paralysed, hungover state, Les knew it was either drown or signal for the lifeguards to come and save his sorry arse, then face the embarrassment of his rescue being televised. Les was about to raise his arm when who should come paddling in his direction, sporting a friendly smile, but Steve Deverell. By the drawn look on Norton's face, Deadline sensed something was amiss, so he paddled straight over and asked Les if he was all right. Les was able to cough and splutter a definite 'No'. So Steve got Norton's ample frame onto his surfboard and paddled him into shore, away from the lifeguards and the *Bondi Rescue* film crew. When he got his breath back, Les thanked Steve profusely and told Deadline he owed him a big one. Get in touch any time and he'd do whatever he could. Now it was time to ante up. Deadline had sent Les an invitation to his wedding, and there was no getting out of it.

Oh well, thought Les, getting up and taking his empty glass out to the kitchen. Steelo should be on his own, so I can hang out with him at the reception. And if Deadline's waxhead mates get too punishing, I'll just make myself scarce. The bottom line is, Steve's a good bloke and I owe him one. So that's that. Les rinsed his glass and placed it in the rack just as a staccato knock sounded on the front door. Les glanced at his watch. I think I know who this might be, he smiled. Les walked up the hallway and opened the door.

Eddie was shuffling around irritably on the welcome mat wearing a blue bomber jacket and a grey T-shirt tucked into a pair of jeans.

'G'day, Eddie,' said Les. 'How are you?'

'All right,' Eddie replied abruptly, walking straight past Norton and down the hallway.

'That's good,' nodded Les.

By the time Les closed the door and followed Eddie down the hallway, Eddie was standing in the loungeroom glaring angrily at him.

'This isn't those fuckin Lebanese arseholes again is it?' he demanded. 'Fair dinkum. If it is, I'll ring Big Arse and sort the dopey wog cunts out once and for fuckin all.'

Les shook his head. 'No. It's not the Lebs, Eddie. They're history. It's something else.'

'Something else?'

'Yeah,' nodded Les. 'I want you to knock a frog for me.'

'A frog?' Eddie's face turned into a sneer. 'You don't mean French Charlie, do you? I know he's full of shit about being in the French Foreign Legion and you had to turf the pain in the arse out of the club the other week. But if he's giving you any grief I'll sort him out. No worries. You'll have to give me a hand to get rid of the body, that's all.'

Les shook his head again. 'No. I don't mean a Frenchman frog, Eddie. I mean …' Les made a tiny gesture cupping his hands together, 'I mean a frog … sort of a frog.'

Eddie tilted his head. 'A frog sort of a frog?' he said. 'You don't mean a … ribet, ribet kind of frog, do you?'

'Yeah,' nodded Les. 'Exactly. A ribet, ribet kind of frog.'

'What!?' Eddie started to smoulder. 'You mean to

tell me, I just left a beautiful latte and a strawberry muffin in Pyrmont, and drove through two fuckin red lights to get here, so I could shoot a fuckin frog?'

'Yeah,' Les nodded weakly.

'Right, that's it. Fuck you, Les.' Eddie whipped a .38 Colt Detective Special from an ankle holster under his jeans and levelled the snub-nosed barrel at Norton's face. 'I'm giving you another nostril, you moron. Right between your fuckin eyes.'

'All right, Eddie,' said Les, making a defensive gesture. 'I don't blame you getting the shits. But please. Just hear me out. This thing is deadset driving me insane.'

Eddie thought for a moment then replaced the gun. 'Okay,' he said. 'But this better be good, I'm tellin you.'

'It is, mate. Believe me.'

'All right.' Eddie nodded to the kitchen. 'Make me a cup of coffee.'

'The coffee machine's stuffed. And Warren's girl broke the plunger. Will a cup of Nescafé with Carnation milk do you?'

'I s'pose it'll have to. Won't it.'

Eddie eased his wiry frame back on a lounge chair while Les sorted things out in the kitchen. There was hot water in the kettle and in no-time Les had two cups of instant coffee together. He handed one to Eddie then sat down on a lounge chair opposite him.

'How's that?' asked Les.

'Pretty good,' replied Eddie, after taking a sip. 'Nothing wrong with a bit of Nescafé now and again.' Eddie took another sip of coffee and looked directly at Les. 'Okay. What's all this about a fuckin frog?'

'Ohh, mate. This is no ordinary frog,' replied Les. 'This is Fabio. The frog from hell.'

Les explained his predicament to Eddie. How he tried to scald the frog, bash it, burn it. But to no avail. And if he didn't get any sleep before long, he'd either blow the house up or throw himself off the Gap. When Les had finished, he expected Eddie to either give him a gigantic verbal or take his gun back out and shoot him as intended. Instead, Eddie was all smiles and understanding.

'Mate,' sympathised Eddie. 'I know exactly what you mean.'

'You do?' said Les.

'Yeah,' nodded Eddie. 'Over in Vietnam. We were at a place called Gia Lai. And the fuckin things there were as big as medicine balls. You could hear them a mile away. Me and Big Barry Benson ended up borrowing a flame thrower off some Yanks one night and gave it to a heap of them before they drove us nuts.'

'Right,' said Les. 'So now you know where I'm coming from.'

'Yep. I'm with you, baby.'

'So can you do something?' pleaded Les.

'Sure, no problem,' smiled Eddie. 'What time does Fabio kick off with his serenading?'

'Mostly nine o'clock. Out in the backyard.'

'Righto. I'll be back here around then. Leave the lights off in the backyard.'

Les reached over and cupped both his hands around one of Eddie's. 'Ohh, God bless you, Eddie. You've restored my sanity.'

'That's all right,' said Eddie. He placed his cup on the coffee table and smiled up at Norton. 'Of course you know this is going to cost you — don't you?'

'Hey. Sweet as,' replied Les. 'Carl Williams was offering three hundred grand for a hit in Melbourne. If that's what you want. No worries.'

Eddie shook his head. 'No. I don't want your money,' he said. 'You're just sitting around picking your arse at the moment like everybody else, aren't you?'

'Pretty much,' agreed Les.

'You know where Nimbin is?'

'Nimbin? Yeah. Up near where I took Peregrine.'

'That's right. It's a long way. But a mate of mine's opening a bar there on the weekend. How about going up Thursday? Give him a hand to sort things out Friday and Saturday night. I'll be up late Saturday. You can come back Sunday morning.'

'Good as gold,' said Les. 'Who's the bloke?'

'Lyle Lonreghan. Lonnie. He's an old mate of mine from Vietnam. He was in the air force.'

'What? A pilot?'

Eddie shook his head. 'No, ground crew. But Lonnie was as good as any soldier I knew. He was a weapons expert. And I mean, expert.'

'Okay,' said Les. 'I'll be there on Thursday.'

Eddie looked at his watch then stood up. 'I got to get going. I'll ring Lonnie, and I'll fill you in a bit more when I see you tonight.'

'Righto.' Les got up and walked Eddie to the door. As he did, he noticed Eddie was limping a little. 'Hey. What's up with your leg?' asked Les.

'Ahh, I was playing squash with George,' answered Eddie, 'and I twisted my bloody ankle.'

'That's no good,' said Les, opening the door. 'Whack plenty of ice on it.'

'Yeah. I have been. It'll be all right in a couple of

days. Hey, I'll tell you what,' said Eddie, taking his keys out. 'The fat cunt's not bad on his feet round a squash court.'

'Yeah. Well, we all know what a good dancer he is,' winked Les.

'Yeah. You're not wrong,' smiled Eddie. 'Okay, I'll see you tonight.'

Eddie walked down and got into his black Mercedes, giving the horn a bip as he drove off. Les waved, closed the door and walked back into the loungeroom.

Lovely, mused Les, taking the two cups into the kitchen. This ties in nicely with the wedding, so I can stop sulking. And you never know. It might turn out to be a bit of fun. You can bet your life if Lonnie's an old mate of Eddie's, he won't be a very solid citizen. Les thought for a moment, smiled, then walked into the loungeroom, found the number he was looking for and dialled.

'Yeah hello.'

'Hello, Deadline. It's Les Norton.'

'Hey,' replied Steve cheerfully. 'How are you, big fellah?'

'All right. So is the wedding still on?'

'Too right, Les. You're definitely coming, aren't you?'

'Are you kidding. I just got my tuxedo out of the cleaners. I can't wait to get there.'

'Unreal.'

'So where are you now?' asked Les.

'Blueys Beach,' answered Steve. 'Sorting things out.'

'Where's Ninety-Nine?'

'I'm not sure. She's supposed to be locked in the tower with the chastity belt on. If I find out she's running with her girlfriends there'll be trouble. Believe me.'

'You're a hard man, Deadline,' said Les.

'You have to be,' said Steve. 'Hey. I'm glad you rang, Les. I need you to do me a favour.'

'No worries. What is it?'

'Steelo's car's shit itself. Can you give him a lift?'

'Sure. I'd be glad to,' replied Les. 'The only thing is, I'm heading on up the coast afterwards to see someone. Can you get him a lift home?'

'Yeah. No sweat,' replied Steve.

'All right. Well, I'll ring Steelo now and tell him what's going on. And I'll see you up there. I'll ring you when we hit town.'

'Okay, big fellah. See you then.'

Les hung up, found another number and dialled.

'Hello.'

'Hello, Tony. It's Les Norton.'

'Hey, Les,' replied the likeable surf photographer. 'How are you, mate?'

'Good. Deadline tells me your car's thrown a wobbly. And you're coming up with me.'

'Yeah. The fuckin brakes went on the fuckin thing. You wouldn't fuckin believe it. Just as I'm about to go away. Fuck it. The motherless fuckin heap of fuckin shit.'

'So what time suits you in the morning, Tony?' asked Les. 'I've never been to Blueys Beach. Or Myall Lakes for that matter.'

'It's only a four-hour drive,' answered Tony. 'How about ten o'clock?'

'Ten o'clock would be perfectly splendid,' beamed Les. 'I'll bip the horn out the front. You just saunter down at your leisure.'

'All right, Les. See you in the morning. And thanks, mate.'

'Steelo. It's my absolute pleasure.'

Les hung up and looked at the phone. You know, it's funny, he mused. I've never heard anyone swear as much as Steelo. And I've never heard one bloke say a bad word about him. Women don't mind him either. Les walked back out to the kitchen and absently rapped his knuckles against the fridge. Okay, he asked himself. What'll I do now?

After wandering around half asleep day after day and night after night, Norton's room needed a good tidy, his sheets needed changing and there were a few other things that could do with a drink. Les shoved everything in the washing machine then cleaned out the car for the trip before driving down to Curlewis Street and filling the tank. By then, the day started to cloud over, making it good for a run, so when he'd finished his domestics, Les climbed into his blue shorts and an old grey T-shirt, got a towel and a sweat rag and strolled down to the beach for a jog on the soft sand.

There weren't many people about and Les didn't have to dodge around any bodies while he did a lazy six laps. He finished with a few crunches and push-ups and as the southerly had picked up didn't bother about a swim to cool off, choosing to walk home and get under a nice steaming hot shower instead. Not long after, Les was seated comfortably in the Hakoah Club wearing a clean pair of jeans, a white T-shirt and a black bomber jacket enjoying a chicken schnitzel with creamy potato salad and vegetables, followed by butterscotch pudding and ice cream, all washed down with a flat white.

By the time Les walked home, dithered around the house and packed what he thought he'd need for Blueys Beach and Nimbin, Monday was well and truly shot. Satisfied he had everything together and the house was secure, Les had a large glass of cold mineral water, climbed into his trackies then settled down in front of the TV to wait for Eddie. After another rotten night's sleep, Les was yawning away, watching not much in particular when there was the same staccato knock on the front door. Les hit the mute button on the TV then strolled down and opened the door. Eddie was standing on the welcome mat, wearing the same clothes as before and carrying a small overnight bag.

'Hello, dude,' said Eddie, stepping inside. 'How are they hanging?'

'Down to my fuckin ankles,' replied Les.

Les closed the door and followed Eddie into the loungeroom. Eddie placed the overnight bag on the lounge and was about to unzip it, when he smiled and cupped a hand behind one ear.

'Hello,' said Eddie. 'Do I hear something?'

From somewhere behind the back verandah came an audible and repetitious 'Pwop! Pwop! Pwop!' Each one louder than the first.

'Yes,' winced Les, 'that's him all right. That's fuckin Fabio.'

'Okay, Fabio,' said Eddie, 'let's see what we've got here for you.'

Eddie opened the bag and took out a short thick object resembling a telephoto lens with a rubber eyepiece and two adjustable straps at one end. He placed it on the lounge, then took out a heavy black pistol with a white serrated handle.

'Shit! What's that?' asked Les, staring at the gun. 'A forty fuckin five? It's twice as big as that thing you shoved in my face this morning.'

'This,' replied Eddie, 'is a Crosman .177 calibre air pistol. It works on a gas cylinder in the front. And a little slot at the back where you drop the pellets in. You cock it by pulling the end back.'

Eddie took a lead pellet from a small plastic box, slipped it in the slot, locked the lever then pulled the end of the gun back. He aimed it at a cushion sitting on a lounge chair across the room and squeezed the trigger. A muffled 'whack' came from the barrel, then the cushion shuddered violently as the pellet thumped into it.

'Holy shit,' exclaimed Les.

'You'd be flat out killing anybody with one of

these,' said Eddie. 'But they'll sit you on your arse pretty quick.'

'I could bloody imagine,' agreed Les, staring over at the hole in his cushion.

Eddie placed the air pistol on the lounge and held up the telephoto lens. 'And this,' he said, 'is an AN/PVS-7 Image Intensifier System. A night vision goggle. Or NVG for short.'

'I've seen those things on TV,' said Les. 'They use them in Iraq and Afghanistan.'

'This one came from Pakistan,' smiled Eddie.

Les gave the NVG a grudging look of approval. 'Fair enough,' he said.

Eddie slipped the NVG on top of his head, then dropped another pellet into the air pistol and locked it in. 'Righto, Les,' he ordered, 'I want you to stay in here and maintain a defence perimeter. I'll perform a strategic forward reconnaissance, positioning myself for a fire and manoeuvre operation.'

'That's an affirmative,' nodded Les.

'Be advised, if I'm not back by twenty-two hundred hours, call in an air strike. On my pod. The co-ordinates are in my bag.'

'Roger — Wilco,' replied Les. 'Delta Foxtrot Charlie. Bravo Company. Over and out.'

Eddie strapped the NVG over one eye. 'Kill them all,' he whispered. 'Kill them all.' Eddie walked out to the verandah, the screen door opened and closed quietly, then, apart from Fabio's serenading, there was silence.

Les sat motionless in front of the mute TV. Out in the backyard he could hear Fabio's constant 'Pwop! Pwop! Pwop!', each burst hitting him like drops in a Chinese water torture. Les was staring absently at the TV, still listening to Fabio's 'Pwop! Pwop! Pwop!' when suddenly a distinct 'Whack!' split the night air, followed by silence. The silence continued before it was abruptly broken by another 'Whack!' Not long after, the screen door opened and Eddie walked into the loungeroom with the air pistol stuffed in the front of his jeans and the NVG in his hand. Dangling by one leg from his other hand were the remains of a small green and brown frog with yellow stripes.

Norton's eyes lit up when he saw the frog. 'You got the cunt,' he said.

Eddie nodded grimly. 'It wasn't easy. His weapon jammed and he came at me with a trench knife. But I managed to overpower him and finish him off with two rounds.'

'Fair dinkum?' said Les. 'It ended up in hand to hand combat. Fuck!'

Eddie placed the gun and the NVG on the lounge then went out to the kitchen. Les followed and watched as Eddie dropped the frog's mangled body on the sink. It had a jagged hole in its back, a bigger one in its stomach and another hole between its eyes. Half its lungs were hanging out of its mouth and a little blood trickled along the sink. However, with his tiny hands spread out in front of him and a dreamy, peaceful look in his bulbous yellow eyes, Fabio still had a cute froggy smile frozen on his face.

'So that's Fabio,' said Les, giving the dead frog a prod with his finger. 'He looks kind of happy. Are you sure he's dead?'

'Am I sure he's dead?' replied Eddie. 'Of course he's fuckin dead. Christ! If you don't believe me, there's a knife in my bag. Stick it in his fuckin ribs.'

'No. I'll take your word for it,' said Les.

Eddie's face hardened. 'The only problem now, Les,' he said seriously, 'is what do we do with the body.'

'Shit! You're right again, Eddie,' answered Les. 'I never thought of that.'

'I can borrow Price's boat,' suggested Eddie. 'And we can take him out the Heads with a couple of car batteries wired to his legs and throw him over the side. That's always worked in the past.'

'It's definitely a thought,' agreed Les. 'Or it might be easier to bury him out near the airport. We've done that before.'

'You got any shovels?'

'Yeah. Out in the shed.'

'I like it,' nodded Eddie. 'We'll take your car.'

Norton looked evenly at Eddie. 'I got a better idea.'

'Whatever turns you on, bro.'

Les picked Fabio up by one leg then took him out to the bathroom and lifted the lid on the toilet. 'Goodbye, you shit of a fuckin thing,' he said, dropping Fabio in the bowl. 'See how many roots you get out the front of Ben Buckler.' Les pushed the flush button and the water swirled, spinning Fabio round in circles a few times before he disappeared forever.

'How did you go?' asked Eddie, when Les walked back into the kitchen.

'Good,' replied Les. 'Fabio got a burial at sea. It was very moving.'

'Wonderful.' Eddie looked at his watch. 'All right. I'd better get going.'

'Righto,' said Les. 'And, Eddie. Thanks, mate. That thing was driving me mad.'

'No worries, Les,' smiled Eddie, patting Les on the shoulder. 'That's what mates are for.'

'I couldn't agree more.' Les followed Eddie into the loungeroom and watched as the deadly hitman replaced everything in his overnight bag. 'So what's the story in Nimbin again?' asked Les.

Eddie handed Les an envelope. 'That's Lonnie's address and phone number. I rang him earlier and told him what's going on. He was rapt. In fact I'll ring him again and you can have a quick word with him.'

'Okay.'

Eddie picked up Norton's land line and dialled. 'Hello. Lonnie. It's Eddie. Yeah. I'm with Les right now. I'll put him on.' Eddie handed Les the phone.

'Hello?'

'Yeah. Is that Les, is it?' came a friendly voice at the other end.

'That's me. How are you, Lyle?'

'I'm good. Call me Lonnie. Everybody else does.'

'Righto, Lonnie.'

'Eddie tells me you're going to come up and give me a hand with the bar for a couple of nights.'

'Yeah. I can sort things out on the door for you. No problems.'

'No. I got a couple of blokes for that. I want you to do the music.'

'Music?' Les was surprised. 'What? Like a DJ?'

'Sort of. I'll explain it to you when I see you.'

'Righto,' shrugged Les.

'You ever been to Nimbin?'

'No,' replied Les.

'Well, when you get here, you may as well book into the pub. Then ring me and let me know everything's sweet.'

'Okay.'

'The bar's called the Double L Ranch. You can't miss it. It's at the end of the main drag, down past the war memorial. I'm opening Friday night at eight. And closing at twelve. The same Saturday. Closed Sunday. I'll give you five hundred a night in the hand. Okay?'

'Sounds good to me, Lonnie,' said Les.

'Okay. Well, I'll see you in Nimbin, Les.'

'See you then, Lonnie.' Les hung up the phone and looked at Eddie.

'Everything sweet?' asked Eddie.

'He wants me to do the music,' replied Les.

'Terrific,' said Eddie, zipping up his overnight bag. 'You like music. It'll be right up your alley.'

'Yeah,' Les nodded absently.

Eddie started off down the hallway. Les followed him and opened the door.

'All right. Ring me when you get a chance,' said

Eddie. 'And I'll see you in beautiful downtown Nimbin.'

'Righto, mate. See you then.'

Eddie walked down to his car and drove off slowly into the night. Les closed the door then walked back into the loungeroom and sat down in front of the silent TV.

Well, that's a trifle odd, thought Les. One would have imagined one would be working on the door, punching people in the face and kicking them in the head when they're down. Instead, this Lonnie bloke wants me to do the music. Les dropped his head into his hands and groaned. Which means I'll be standing in front of a steaming turntable playing fuckin house music all night. Great. I get rid of one horrible racket and walk straight into another. Oh well. It's only for two nights. And between the money and Eddie doing me a huge favour, I can't whinge.

Les cocked an ear towards the backyard and the beautiful silence was blissfully deafening. Suddenly Norton was overcome by a strange mixture of blessed relief and total exhaustion. Fuckin hell, he yawned to himself. This is too good to be true. I'm hitting the sack. Les rinsed Fabio's blood from the sink, turned off the TV and the lights and shuffled down to his darkened bedroom.

The bed felt extraordinarily comfortable and the clean fresh sheets and pillowcases were a delight. The silence outside his window was a revelation. Les gave a sigh of happiness, smiled and scrunched his head into the pillows. Next thing his eyes rolled back in his head and in seconds the big redheaded Queenslander was snoring like a baby.

It was well past nine when Norton woke up the next morning and after a long night of undisturbed sleep, Les felt like a new man. He got out of bed, stretched, smiled and breezed down the hallway to the bathroom. A check of his face while he cleaned his teeth told Les the winning sparkle had returned to his beautiful brown eyes and the nasty black circles had already started to clear up.

'Hello, you magnificent, gorgeous hunk of Australian manhood,' he smiled, blowing himself a kiss in the mirror. 'And how are you today? What's that? You feel great. Goodness! I wonder why?' Les filled a glass with water and toasted the toilet bowl. 'To absent friends,' he said, then drained the glass.

It was a clear crisp day outside and although he was off to a late start, Norton knew there was no way in the world Tony Nathan would be ready and waiting out the front when he drove round. So, after slipping into a pair of blue cargoes, his AND1 trainers and a blue T-shirt with coloured fish on it that he'd bought in Cairns, Les strolled down to Hall Street to get the paper, stopping on the way home for a flat white at the corner café.

Back at Chez Norton, Les cooked enough scrambled eggs and bacon to end world hunger, then lingered over the news again with his instant coffee. Full as a tick, he folded his newspaper, cleaned up, then put his bags in the car; Warren would be home that evening, so there was no need to tell the neighbours he was going away. Satisfied everything was in order for the trip north, Les locked the front door, got into his car and drove round to Tony's flat at Tamarama, pulling up along the driveway next door. Les turned off the motor, bipped the horn and waited.

After enough time to build both the Suez Canal and the Great Pyramid of Cheops, Tony appeared out the front wearing a pair of grey shorts and a black polo shirt. In one hand was a black briefcase, a blue overnight bag hung from his shoulder, and he was eating a banana. Finishing the banana he ambled nonchalantly across to Norton's Berlina.

'Toss your gear on the back seat,' said Les, reaching behind him and opening the rear door.

Tony did that then strolled around and got in the front seat with his briefcase. He placed it on his knees, clicked the seat belt then turned to Les. 'So, what's doing, Shitbags?' he smiled from beneath a mop of thick black hair.

'Not much, Tony,' replied Les. 'What's doing with you?'

'Work. Nothing but fuckin work,' answered Tony. 'And that's about fuckin it. You looking forward to the wedding?'

'Yeah. It should be good,' said Les, starting the car. He nodded to the briefcase as they drove off up the hill. 'What have you got there. The NATO battle plans?'

'No. It's a laptop fuckin computer. The prick of a thing. Fair dinkum. They're enough to drive you round the fuckin bend.'

'So what did you bring it for?' asked Les.

'I've got to match up all these photos and other assorted fuckin shit,' replied Tony. 'So I thought I'd try and get it done while we're driving.' He flipped the laptop open and turned it on.

'Fair enough,' said Les. 'I'll leave the stereo off.'

'No. Don't worry about it,' said Tony. 'I can still work the dopey fuckin thing out.' Tony glared at the screen as he scrolled up and down. 'Some fuckin how.'

'Okay. I might just listen to the news.'

Les switched the radio on down low and while Tony clicked, clattered and abused his laptop, surfed the airwaves. After listening to the usual shock jocks and schlock jocks on AM, Les switched to FM. The first song he got was The Eagles' 'Hotel California' for the two hundred thousandth time on one station, followed by Johnny Farnham wailing 'Help' on another, followed by some unintelligible hip-hop junk on another. This was topped off on another station by an old Englebert Humperdinck song that refused to die, so Les switched the radio off and concentrated on the drive.

By the time they got onto the F3 and crossed the Hawkesbury River, Les found he was having more fun thinking about the funny side of life and watching Tony swear and threaten to murder his laptop than he would listening to old pop songs. Time and the kilometres flew by. Les had drunk a bottle of water and was still chuckling quietly to himself when Tony switched off his computer and slammed it shut.

'That's it. Fuck it,' he cursed. 'Useless cunt of a thing. I'd like to throw it out the fuckin window.'

'You get everything done?' asked Les.

Tony shook his head. 'No. I still got plenty to go. Fuckin enter. Delete. Tools. Fuckin format. Drives me fuckin mad.' Tony looked out the window at the plains and trees on either side of the road. 'Shit! Where the fuck are we?'

'The other side of Hexham. We're heading for Bulahdelah.'

'Shit! That went quick.'

'Yeah. You know what they say, Steelo. Time flies when you're having fun.'

Tony reached behind him and got a bottle of water from his bag. He took a drink then smiled at Norton. 'So, you're looking forward to the wedding are you, Les?'

'Yeah. I like Deadline and his girl.'

'There could be a bit of fun and games at the reception,' chuckled Tony.

'How do you mean?' asked Les.

'You know anything about Deadline and Saretta's background?'

'Background? No. What's there to know?'

'Well,' said Tony, 'Deadline's family are Serbian. And Ninety-Nine's are Bosnian. Evidently there's a blood feud between the two families that goes back five hundred years.'

'Yeah?' Les was surprised. 'So how come they got together and produced bonnie babies?'

'I don't know,' shrugged Tony. 'Deadline originally comes from Tuncurry. Saretta comes from Bondi. They met at an *Off Shore* party at the Bronte Inn. After that it was love all the way. Shit happens.'

'So you're not about to tell me they're going to pull out guns, knives and dynamite at the reception, are you, Steelo?' said Les.

'I doubt it,' replied Tony. 'But if they ramp up on too much plum brandy, you never know what might happen.'

'Shit! Well, if the place goes off, I'll be on the toe very smartly, Tony, I can promise you that,' said Les.

Tony rubbed his hands together. 'You and I might be in for a bit of fun and games up there too, Les.'

'Oh?'

'The boys from *Off Shore* are having dinner at the Lakes tonight.'

'The Lakes?' said Les.

'Yeah. The Lakes Sailing Club,' replied Tony. 'It's like the local RSL. And I know a little chick there that works in the bistro.'

'You do?'

'Yeah, Ruby. The Redhead. I used to take her out in Sydney. Fair dinkum. She's got long red hair down to her knees and legs up to her armpits.'

'Sounds good,' said Les. 'So where do I come into it?'

'She's got a girlfriend works there, Janet. Janet the Gannet from the Forbidden Planet. We've a chance of getting them back to the flat for a drink tonight.'

'So you put in a bit of groundwork before you left, Steelo.'

'Fuckin oath,' enthused Tony. 'I'm still sweet with Ruby. And I reckon even a big ugly gorilla like you would have to be a chance with Janet.'

'Thanks, Steelo,' grunted Les. 'You're too fuckin kind.'

They continued on, crossing the Karuah River when Tony wrinkled his nose and stared at Norton.

'Jesus fuckin Christ, Les,' he said. 'What have you been eating? Curried rat?'

'What do you mean?' asked Les.

'You just farted, you cunt,' said Tony, winding down his window.

Les shook his head. 'It's not me. It's the bloke that used to own the car.'

'What?'

Les explained how the car belonged to a drug dealer who got shot in the car and some of his brains got spattered around the back. With the help of a mechanic they got the smell out. But for some reason it had started seeping back now and again.

'Even though the old Berlina still goes all right,' said Les, 'I got to get another car. I'm spewing.'

'You're not the only one,' said Steelo, poking his face out the window.

They continued on through a warren of roadworks till they came to a sign saying BULAHDELAH. POPULATION 1161. They passed the turn-off to the small township and further on reached the Lakes Way. Route 6. Seal Rocks. Smiths Lake. Pacific Palms.

Tony pointed to the sign. 'There it is, Les.'

'Yep,' nodded Les. 'Time to hang a mean right.'

Les turned off the F3 and past another sign saying TUNCURRY, FORSTER, the road narrowed and began to climb and curve before dipping down again with a steep drop away on the left. They passed a clutter of houses and a store near a sign saying BOOLAMBAYTE then there was a glimpse of lake and they were in the thick of Myall Lakes National Park. Past Bungwahl the lake opened up on the right and further on it almost came up to the road before a row of shops and houses went past on the left near the State Emergency Services building and a sign that read WELCOME TO PACIFIC PALMS. The road rose then dipped and before long Tony pointed to another sign and a turn-off on the right that read BLUEYS BEACH, BOOMERANG BEACH.

'There it is, Les. Blueys Beach.'

Les touched the brakes. 'Don't worry, Steelo. I'm on the case.'

Les hung a right and they followed a narrow road with steep hills and houses on the right and trees and plains on the left. A kilometre further on the left, they came to the little shopping village and parking area of Blueys Beach, separated from the road and the houses opposite by a row of palm trees. Les slowed down and swung the car into the parking area.

'We got to find Blueys Real Estate,' said Tony, 'and pick up the key.'

'There it is. Next to the surf shop. There's a parking spot in front of that phone box.'

'Righto. I'll sort things out. I shouldn't be too long.'

'No. Of course not,' said Les.

Les nosed the Berlina up against the phone box and cut the engine. Tony got out and walked into the real estate office while Les strolled off towards the left to check out the small but well-contained village.

At the end was another real estate agency next to a bakery then a surf shop and Blueys Real Estate, where Les could see Tony smiling away at a young blonde girl behind the desk. Several people were standing inside a takeaway fish and chip shop and a handful of people were drinking coffee under umbrellas outside a café called Fifty-Fifty that sat next to a pizza shop named Louie's on Blueys. Last of the shops was a supermarket and a little further on was a large bottle shop with a parking area out the front. There was a smattering of people getting in and out of cars and several tradies' utes were parked around the fish and chip shop. On the way back, Les stopped outside Fifty-Fifty and had a look inside. Around the tables the walls were stacked with gourmet foods, the kitchen was at the rear and behind the counter a large photo of Blueys Beach took up part of the wall. Les checked a menu on one of the tables and gave it a grudging nod of approval. Yes. I think this is where one shall breakfast tomorrow morning with the paper. And if Steelo can drag his arse out of bed, he's more than welcome to join me. My dollar.

Back at Blueys Real Estate, Tony was still inside chatting up the girl behind the desk, who was batting her eyes and returning his smiles with interest. Les leaned his backside against the bonnet of the car and waited. Finally Tony came out holding a plastic folder and a small map.

'Everything sweet?' Les asked.

'Yep. We're in San Remo apartments.' Tony pointed past the shops. 'Just up the road. A minute's walk to the beach.'

'Beautiful,' said Les. 'We'll dump our gear. Then come back and get some piss for tonight. If it's on?'

'Don't worry.' Tony wiggled his eyebrows at Les. 'If it's not, the little chick in the real estate just gave me her phone number.'

'You were in there long enough. It's a wonder she didn't give herself lockjaw.'

'Shut up, Les, you ugly big cunt,' smiled Tony as they got back inside the car, 'and get us up to the flat.'

Les started the car and stared at Tony. 'Are you any relation to Warren Edwards?'

'No. But your relationship with the rent is two hundred and twenty bucks. So cough up, Shitbags. Unless you want to sleep in the car.'

Les drove left out of the village then took a street to the right. San Remo flats were a large holiday resort that took up a hilly corner on the left. The entrance was just round the corner in a street surrounded by new houses built onto a headland overlooking Blueys Beach.

'Why don't we check out the beach first?' suggested Les.

'Yeah. Good idea,' said Tony.

Les stopped the car at an open-air shower in front of a few scrubby trees surrounded by holiday homes. They got out and walked down a short flight of steps to a wooden viewing platform overlooking a beach a little longer than Coogee, but not as long as Bondi.

'Shit! How nice is this?' said Les.

'Yeah,' agreed Tony. 'Check out the water.'

A rugged granite headland, with houses built onto the green slopes above, ran alongside the ocean on the left and an expanse of white sand led to another headland on the right, where the granite cliffs continued on to Seal Rocks in the distance. New houses and holiday homes overlooked the ocean, finishing where lush forest sloped down to the beach. The water was turquoise blue, there was a mid tide, the breeze was a light south-wester and the only signs of life were a couple walking along the sand and a handful of surfers at the southern end of the beach.

'Shit! I could live here,' declared Tony.

'Yeah. Look at that,' said Les. 'At Bondi, you're competing for a bit of space. Here, you just make your own.'

Tony shook his head. 'Come on, let's head for the flat before I get the shits. This is too fuckin nice.'

San Remo flats were two white stucco blocks, facing each other across a long parking area and built Mexican style with arched entrances and colonnades. Behind the flats were lawns and barbecues edged by small trees running along a steep slope that separated the flats from the road. Les and Tony were on the second floor of the block closest to the entrance.

'Viva Espana,' winked Les.

'Yeah. Hasta la vista, baby,' replied Tony.

The stairs to their flat ran up alongside the building to a small verandah overlooking the parking area. They got their bags from the car and took the stairs. Tony opened the door and they stepped inside.

'Hey, nothing wrong with this,' said Tony.

'Not bad at all, Steelo,' said Les. 'You done well.'

Their holiday apartment was a bright two-bedroom unit painted light blue and white. A blue floral bamboo lounge sat opposite a well-appointed kitchen on the right, a room with a double bed faced the lounge and a room with two single beds and a bunk faced the kitchen. Across from the lounge was a TV and across from the kitchen was the bathroom and behind the kitchen another door opened onto a sundeck overlooking the lawned area. The unit had a polished wooden floor and small colourful seascapes dotted the walls.

'Which bedroom do you want, Steelo?' asked Les.

'I don't give a fuck,' answered Tony. 'You may as well take the double bed. Your arse is twice as big as mine.'

'So are my fists, Brillo Head. So don't get too fuckin smart. All right. I'll take the double bed.'

Norton's room had a closet in the corner and a set of drawers against the wall on the right. A window opened onto the parking area and the checked duvet matched the light blue walls. The only problem was the bed. It was on rollers and when Les tried it out, it took off towards the window. When he stood up and tossed his overnight bag on it, the bed rolled towards the wall. Bloody hell, thought Les. If I toss around in my sleep tonight, I'll finish up on the balcony. He took his shaving kit out and put it in the bathroom, then placed his ghetto blaster on top of the drawers and switched it on, finding a local FM station playing Fleetwood Mac 'You Make Loving Fun'. It was a cruisy old tune with a laid back beat and echoed smoothly around the flat.

'All right, Tony,' said Les, peering into Tony's room. 'We going round to get some piss?'

Tony looked up from what he was doing. 'Yeah righto. I'll just go to the bathroom.'

Les found a large glass in the kitchen, poured himself a drink of water and settled down on the lounge to wait for Tony. Tony eventually got his act and his credit cards together and stepped into the loungeroom.

'Righto, Shitbags,' he said. 'Let's go.'

'Yes. Why don't we.' Les took his glass out to the kitchen, turned off the ghetto blaster and they walked down to the car.

The large bottle shop had an extensive variety of imported beers and spirits. There was a crushed-ice box and at one end was a servery full of pickles and snacks. Les bought a six-pack of Becks, a six-pack of Carlton long necks, a bottle of Jack Daniel's and a bottle of Stolichnaya vodka. Plus a bag of ice, sparkling mineral water and a tub of grilled eggplant. Tony got two six-packs of Jack Daniel's and Coke, two six-packs of Bacardi Cruisers and two large packets of corn chips. Les settled his share of the rent with Tony, then back at the flat, they crammed everything into the fridge and stared at each other.

'Christ,' said Tony. 'Are you sure we bought enough piss?'

'Yeah. I don't think we're going to run short,' agreed Les. 'So what's your John Dory now, Steelo?'

'My story? Fuck round on my laptop and try and finish what I started in the car.'

'Okay.' Les looked at his watch. 'Well, the day's about rooted. I'm going for a run on the beach before it gets dark.'

'Fair enough,' smiled Tony, taking a can of Jackie's and Coke from the fridge. 'Enjoy.'

'Thanks. I will.' Les changed into his training gear, wrapped an old sweat rag around his head then slipped into a pair of thongs and walked down to Blueys Beach.

The breeze was a gentle off-shore when he got there and a smattering of amethyst-tinged clouds were drifting across the sky towards the horizon, while a lone sea eagle floated above the northern headland. A cluster of seagulls sat patiently at the water's edge facing into the wind and the two surfers left at the south end were enjoying the late session. Yes, smiled Norton, taking it all in. This will do me admirably. Leaving his towel and thongs by the water's edge, Les happily jogged off.

Thinking about this, that and the other, Les did eight laps and it was pure enjoyment not having to dodge around people or worry about what might be sticking up out of the sand. He finished with a series of crunches then had a quick dip in the clear blue ocean followed by a freshwater shower at the top of the steps. Back at the flat, Tony was seated on a bar stool in the kitchen abusing his laptop. He looked up when Les walked in with his towel around his shoulders.

'How was the run?'

'Grouse. The water was all right too.' Les had two glasses of tap water, then half a bottle of sparkling mineral water. 'So how are you going, Tony?' Les belched. 'You get everything finished?'

'Yeah. Just about,' replied Tony. 'Except this motherless cunt of a thing has nearly driven me mad.'

'Don't stress out, Steelo,' smiled Norton. 'You'll be sweet.' He took off his sweatband. 'Okay. I'm going to have a Dad 'n Dave and an Eiffel Tower.'

'Terrific,' said Tony, glaring daggers at his laptop.

Les showered and shaved and hung his wet training gear on the back verandah. After changing into his blue cargoes and a grey North Bondi Life Savers T-shirt, he ran a bug rake through his hair then walked out to the kitchen and took an icy cold long neck from the fridge.

'You want a beer or something, Tony?' he asked.

Tony looked up from his laptop. 'Yeah, why not,' he answered. 'Give us a can of JD and Coke. I'm finished here. Fuck it.'

Les hooked the ring-pull off a can of JD and handed it to Tony, then sat down on a bar stool and watched as Tony closed his laptop and took a drink. 'Now, what's the story again tonight, Steelo?' asked Les.

'We'll have dinner at the club. Say hello to Deadline and the boys. Then you and I shall sneak off and await the arrival of Ruby and Janet.'

'So it's definitely on?'

'Yep. I rang the Redhead earlier. And we're looking good.'

'How far is it to the club?' asked Les.

'About five clicks. I can get Deadline to arrange for the courtesy bus if you want,' suggested Tony. 'Save you driving.'

Les shook his head. 'No. I'll take it easy on the piss. Then give it a giant nudge when we get back. I'm in no hurry to get up in the morning.'

'Fair enough.' Tony took another pull at his can of JD, almost draining it. 'All right,' he belched. 'I'm going to have a scrub.'

Les pointed his bottle towards the bathroom. 'The shower's good. There's heaps of hot water.'

'Good.'

Les switched on the TV and waited for Tony. He watched the news, current affairs, finished his long neck, and was half getting interested in a real-life cops show when Tony stepped out of his bedroom wearing a pair of black shorts and a yellow polo shirt. He walked across to the fridge and got another can of JD, then sat down in the lounge near Les, smelling of good aftershave.

'Anything worth watching on TV?' asked Tony, taking a healthy swig from his can.

'Not really.' Les looked evenly at Tony. 'You want to get going, Steelo? I'm fuckin starving.'

'Yeah, me too. I'll finish this in the car.'

Les switched off the TV, Tony locked the flat and they walked down to the Berlina.

The Sailing Club was a short, winding drive back towards Forster with the lake on the left. Sitting across from a cluster of houses built into the surrounding hills, the single storey club was obscured at the front by latticework and trees and the entrance was at the rear. Les parked the car, Tony dumped his empty can into a garbage bin, then they walked over to a short flight of steps leading into a blue-carpeted foyer. After Les signed his temporary membership form, he noticed on the walls of the corridor running down to an auditorium, framed, autographed posters of groups that had played the club: the Whitlams, the John Butler Trio, Machine Gun Fellatio and others. Taking pride of place above a doorway was the legendary Billy Thorpe.

Les followed Tony through a glass door on the left into a spacious dining room with a bank of TV screens beaming down on several rows of long grey tables near the windows on the left. The tables faced the bistro and another glass door on the right, next to a sweets machine, led to the bar and gambling area. Seated haphazardly along the tables below the TV sets were Steve Deverell and his waxhead mates, mostly wearing jeans, shorts and T-shirts. Some had their wives and girlfriends with them and several kids were giggling and running around the tables. There was a great hoo-ha of greetings, abuse and laughter when Tony walked in with Les, indicating everybody was glad to see their photographer mate.

'Hello. It's Thelma and Louise,' said Steve, sitting a little away from the others, wearing a white T-shirt with TAHITI on the front. 'How are you, Steelo, you miserable cunt? You got here.'

'Yeah. Just to fuckin annoy you, Deadline. You great goose,' replied Tony.

'G'day, Les,' Steve smiled up at Norton.

'Hello, Deadline.' Les returned Steve's smile and stepped over to shake his hand. 'Congratulations.'

'Thanks, mate. And thanks for coming.'

'I wouldn't have missed it for the world, Steve.'

'You want a drink, Les?' asked Tony.

'Yeah. That'd be good. Get us a schooner of lite, will you, mate.'

Tony disappeared towards the bar and Les sat down alongside Steve. 'So how's it going, Deadline?' asked Les.

Steve shook his head. 'Ohh, I don't know, mate. It's my last night as a free man.'

'It's not too late, you know. I can put you in the boot of the car and have you over the Queensland border by morning.'

'I was thinking of stealing a kayak, paddling across the lake and hiding out in the bush. But the in-laws'd hunt me down like a mangy dog.'

'What about a helicopter snatch at the last minute, Steve?' suggested Les. 'Eddie could organise that.'

'Shit! Now that's an idea,' said Steve. 'In the meantime, Les, meet some of my mad mates.'

'Righto.'

Steve stood up, Les did the same and Steve introduced Les around. Steve's mates were a fit, tanned, happy-go-lucky bunch of larrikins with warm handshakes and smiles to match. Some were a little wary of Norton's gangster reputation, but they soon made him feel right at home. They all had names like Roy Boy, Ray, Mitch, Oaksy, Fletch etc. The standout was a tall wiry bloke with a happy face under a shock of unruly blond hair, who Steve introduced as Cunzdrug. Cunzdrug roamed around the tables joking and horsing about and every time someone called out his name, it sounded like they were calling him Cunt Struck. Tony arrived back with Norton's schooner and a middy for himself. Les thanked him and, still a little dry from the run, had no trouble putting almost half of it away in one swallow.

'You ready to eat, Les?' asked Tony.

'Am I what,' belched Les. He put his beer down and followed Tony over to the bistro.

An appetising aroma of grilled meat drifted out from the kitchen into the servery. Sitting on the glass counter was a bowl of lemons; Les pocketed two for the Jack Daniel's and mineral water when he got home. Standing behind the servery was a stocky girl in her late twenties with a mane of copper-coloured hair tucked up under a white cap. She had full red lips and cheeky onyx eyes, oozed oomph and was stacked in all the right places beneath her black uniform. As soon as she spotted Tony her eyes lit up and a wide grin spread across her face.

'Tony,' she squealed. 'How are you, you sweet gorgeous thing?'

'Unreal, Ruby darling,' smiled Tony. 'How are you?'

Ruby closed her eyes and placed her hands over her heart. 'How do you think I am, Tony. I see you and my heart skips a beat.'

'I see you, Ruby,' grinned Tony, 'and something I got snaps to attention.'

'Oooh, Tony,' breathed Ruby, 'you are awful.'

'Ruby. This is my mate Les I was telling you about.'

Ruby gave Les a quick and approving once-up-and-down. 'Hello, Les,' she said. 'How are you?'

'Good thanks, Ruby,' smiled Les. 'Nice to meet you.'

'So what time are you coming round tonight? Is everything sweet?' asked Tony.

'Yes. Janet's in the kitchen and we both finish at ten. By the time we clean up and have a quick staffie, ten-thirty.'

'Can you get home all right afterwards? I fancy having a few drinks.'

'No worries. We'll get a taxi over and Janet's cousin does night security. He'll drive us home.'

'Beauty,' said Tony. 'Okay. I'm going to have a T-bone steak. What about you, Les?'

'You got me, Steelo,' replied Les. 'A T-bone sounds good.'

'All right, Ruby, hustle us up the two biggest T-bones you got. With chips and salad and pepper sauce. Pepper sauce do you, Les?'

'Perfect,' smiled Les. 'I'll shout. What do we owe you, Ruby?'

Les paid the bill, Tony picked up the buzzer then they rejoined Steve while they waited for their food.

Rather than join in any conversation, Les was happy to sit back and listen to Steve's mates and found himself pleasantly surprised. There was no inane waxhead talk like the grommets down on Bondi Beach. Steve's friends were photographers and journalists. Some worked in computers. Two had written books. One had a furniture business. A tall, dark-haired bloke named Errol was a pilot and had just spent six months travelling and surfing around the Pacific. Errol had some great anecdotes to relate about people living on tiny islands most of the world never knew existed. Eventually the buzzer went off and Les and Tony walked over and picked up their meals.

Ruby certainly looked after them with the steaks — they were huge and flame-grilled to perfection. The chips were golden brown, there was plenty of crisp fresh salad with a tangy dressing, and she'd shouted them garlic bread. Les and Tony ripped in till there was nothing left except the bones and the alfoil the garlic bread came in. When they'd finished, Les didn't feel like another beer and neither did Tony. Around them Steve and his mates were starting to rev up with most of the banter directed at Deadline and Cunzdrug, who managed to return serve with reprehensible panache. Les was chuckling away at their antics when Tony pulled him aside and tapped his watch.

'We'd better make a move,' he said. 'It's not getting any earlier.'

'Fair enough,' agreed Les.

Tony turned to Steve. 'We have to get going,' said Tony. 'We'll see you tomorrow at the wedding.'

'You're leaving us?' said Steve.

Cunzdrug picked up on this. 'Hey, Thelma and Louise,' he called out. 'You're not going already, are you?'

'We have to, Cunt Struck,' said Les. 'Tony wants to iron his dress for tomorrow. And I've got to sew a strap on my evening gown.'

'Beautiful,' smiled Cunzdrug.

'That's exactly how we intend to look,' Les smiled back.

Les shook hands with Steve and a couple of his mates, then to a round of catcalls and good-natured banter, Les and Tony made their exit. Back in the car, Les started the engine and turned to Tony.

'Well, what a friendly bunch of blokes,' he said. 'Deadline's sure got some good buddies.'

'Ohh, mate,' replied Tony. 'You want to try working with the cunts. Or take a trip to Indo with them. You're in stitches the whole time.'

Les reversed out then nosed the car towards the exit. As he did, a police car pulled in behind them and drove into the parking area.

'Holy fuck!' said Les. 'Look at that. I knew I was better off taking it easy on the piss.'

'Ahh, you'd have been right,' said Tony. 'They weren't interested in you.'

Les shook his head. 'That's not how it works if you're driving over the limit, Steelo,' he said, turning right onto the road back home. 'You can be the safest driver in the world, but if some dill runs into you, you're ratshit.'

Tony thought for a moment. 'You know, you're right,' he agreed. 'My mate Pete was driving home one night, just a little bit over the limit. And some sheila on a mobile phone ran up his arse. The cops came and Pete finished up doing his licence for three months. Plus a fine and the insurance company told him to get fucked.'

'See, Tony,' said Norton. 'Listen to your uncle Les and you can't go wrong.'

Back at the flat, Les beat Tony to the toilet then made himself a massive Jackie's and soda with a slice of lemon. He placed the ghetto blaster on top of the TV and while he sipped his Jack Daniel's in the loungeroom and listened to Richard Clapton crooning 'Girls on the Avenue' on FM, contemplated his blind date. Tony appeared out of the bathroom, took a Jackie's and Coke from the fridge, opened a packet of corn chips and sat down in the lounge across from Les.

'Fair dinkum, Steelo,' said Les. 'This Janet the Gannet from the Forbidden Planet better not be too ugly. Or the next photos you take will be from a hospital bed.'

'Mate. Don't shit yourself,' Tony replied easily. 'I know her. She's not a bad sort. Anyway. You're not Orlando Bloom. So get fucked.'

'Thanks. So where do you know the two lovelies from?' asked Les.

'Sydney. They used to work at the pub up from *Off Shore*.' Tony wiggled his eyebrows. 'Me and the redhead have been friends for ages. And here. Take these.' Tony fished into his pocket and tossed Les two condoms.

'Frenchies,' said Les.

'Yeah. You never know your luck, Orlando,' smiled Tony.

'Fair enough,' said Les, putting them in his pocket.

More Jackie's went down and more music played. Les was getting a glow on and starting to think something might have gone wrong when lights flashed in the parking area below. Tony walked across to the open door and had a look.

'They're here,' he grinned, and went back to his seat.

'Be still my beating heart,' said Les.

The car drove off, followed by laughter and voices coming up the stairs, then Ruby walked in followed by a tall, whippy brunette with a mop of frizzy brown hair.

She had a lean, happy face, not short of a freckle or two, cheeky green eyes and a soft mouth stretched across slightly bucked teeth. Slung across her shoulder was a black leather handbag and tucked into a pair of baggy blue shorts hugging her wasp waist was a white V-necked angora jumper. Ruby was carrying a denim handbag and had changed into a black Rolling Stones T-shirt over a pair of jeans. The sleeves of a grey hooded jacket hung loosely round her neck and Tony wasn't joking about Ruby's hair. It shone like polished brass and tumbled all the way down to her shapely backside. As soon as she spotted Tony, she jiggled happily across the room and planted a big kiss on his lips.

'Hello, darling,' she grinned. 'How are you, my dearest treasure?'

'Unreal, Red,' Tony grinned back. 'Unreal.' He left Ruby then stepped over, grabbed Janet and planted a big kiss on her mouth. 'Hello, Janet, you big spunk,' he smiled wolfishly. 'How long's it been?'

'Ohh, too long, fellah. Too long,' laughed Janet. 'Where have you been?'

'Stuck in bloody Sydney.' Tony let go of Janet and turned to Norton. 'Janet. This is my friend Les. Les, meet Janet the Gannet from the Forbidden Planet.'

'Hello, Janet. Nice to meet you,' smiled Les, standing up and offering his hand.

Janet gave Les a quick once-up-and-down before shaking his hand. 'Hello, Les,' she said cheerfully, evidently liking what she saw. 'Nice to meet you too.'

'My pleasure, Janet,' smiled Les.

Tony rubbed his hands together. 'Okay. Who wants what?'

'What have you got?' asked Ruby.

'Plenty,' replied Tony.

'I'll tell you what,' cut in Les. 'You girls have been working hard all night. Why don't you put your feet up and let me be the drink waiter. You too, Steelo. You've had a hard day at the laptop. Allow me.'

'Go for your life, Stooge,' said Tony.

The girls placed their bags on the table, Tony moved up next to Ruby while Les did his best to play the perfect host. Ruby went for a vodka and ice with a Bacardi Cruiser chaser, Janet chose a Jack Daniel's and ice and a Becks chaser, Tony settled for another can of Jackie's while Les poured himself another monster delicious. After that, the night went swimmingly.

Janet loved a drink and it turned out she was a Kiwi with a 'thuck' Kiwi accent that matched her zany sense of humour, and came from a little town in the South Island of New Zealand. Life in Australia was good, Sydney was a great town, but living on the north coast bordered somewhere between 'fenntestuck' and 'febbulous' and the pay working as an assistant chef at the Sailing Club wasn't bad either. She met Ruby on a skiing trip to Thredbo and knew Steve and all his waxhead mates when she and Janet worked in the hotel where the boys from *Off Shore* used to drink after work. She got the nickname Janet the Gannet from the Forbidden Planet because she was a mad science fiction fan and loved books and movies about outer space — the older and cornier the better. Les told Janet pretty much the truth about himself: he came from a little town in Queensland, owned a house in Bondi and worked at a club in Kings Cross that could be quite a heavy scene at times. He and Tony were mates from Bondi and they were up at Blueys for their mutual friend Steve's wedding. Like Janet, he agreed Sydney was a great town. But it was just as great to get away every now and again and one day he intended buying a home, probably up the north coast somewhere, and putting his feet up. In that respect, there was nothing wrong with what he'd seen of Blueys Beach so far. Particularly the steaks at the Sailing Club.

'Honestly, Les,' said Janet, after copious Jack Daniel's and Becks chasers, 'you've got to get an old black-and-white movie made in the fifties, *Teenagers from Outer Space*.'

'*Teenagers from Outer Space*?' said Les.

'Yes,' nodded Janet. 'These Elvis lookalikes in a Chevy convertible have got a ray gun, and when they zap people with it, all their skin melts away leaving just their skeletons. And the skeletons have got hooks on their skulls and storage numbers written across their ribs. The spaceship's made out of air-conditioning ducts and hub caps. It's a deadset crecck up.'

'When I get home,' promised Les, 'I'll make sure the local video shop orders it in. And my flatmate and myself shall watch it with avid interest.'

The happy quartet binge-drinked on into the night while the local FM station churned out plenty of old rock songs. Les and Janet were getting on famously while Tony and Ruby were climbing all over each other on the lounge. Les looked away for a few moments and when he looked back, Tony had Ruby by the hand and was leading her into the bedroom. The door closed leaving Les and Janet alone in the loungeroom.

'Looks like we've lost Tony and Ruby's company,' smiled Les.

'Yes. It certainly looks that way,' Janet smiled back.

Les enjoyed Janet's company; she was fun. But the drive, the run, the big meal and the sudden, late intake of booze had taken the edge off Norton and he wasn't quite in the mood for a long round of heavy seduction before getting into a bout of porking. But under all the hair, Janet had a wild, sexy look about her and she sported a great pair of legs. So Les was going to have to make some sort of an effort or she might get offended. Les took a sip of his delicious and gave Janet another smile.

'Janet,' said Les, placing his hand on her knee, 'I don't quite know how to put this, but I'll do my best.'

'Okay, Les,' replied Janet. 'Do your best, fellah.'

Les patted Janet's knee. 'If I hit on you, and try to get into your pants, it's sexual harassment. And I'm regarded as no more than a drunken, sex-crazed Australian yobbo. Right?'

'That's exactly right, Les,' nodded Janet.

'But you're a horny big thing, Janet. And if I don't make some sort of a move while I'm still able to, you'll think there's something wrong with me. Or worse, I'm a horse's hoof.'

'That's right too, Les,' said Janet, jiggling the ice in her glass. 'You can't win, fellah.'

'So I'll get straight to the point.' Les nodded towards his bedroom. 'I've got all the rubber we need. Do you want to hop in the sack and get into a bit of good old-fashioned porking? Yes or no, Janet? It's up to you.'

Janet took another drink then smiled at Les over her glass. 'How about I give your dick a wee suck first.'

'Well ...' said Les. 'If you insist. Why not?'

His tiredness suddenly abating, Les put his drink down, then led Janet across to the bedroom and closed the door behind them. Janet got down to a pair of plain white knickers about the same time Les got down to his jox, and Janet was out of her underwear the same time Les was out of his. She had a neat body, tight boobs and a bristly ted jutted out beneath her navel like a little pine cone. Mr Wobbly had sniffed the wind and as soon as he realised there was action in the air, rose menacingly to the occasion. Janet took hold of Norton's balls, then eased her backside down on the edge of the bed to get Mr Wobbly in her mouth, when she let out a little squeal as the bed took off beneath her, landing under the window where she knocked the back of her head against the sill.

'Holy shit!' said Janet, rubbing her head. 'What's going on?'

'It's the bed,' explained Les. 'It's on rollers.'

'Bloody hell! This is going to be fun.'

'It'll be all right, Janet. I promise. Don't worry.'

Janet sat back up on the bed and Les moved towards it, stopping the bed from moving by jamming his legs against the side, then Janet got to work on Mr Wobbly. And Janet was good. She sucked and licked and gnawed at his shiny pink head with her buck teeth, sending shivers up and down Norton's spine. Janet knew she was good, too. While she was polishing merrily away she'd give Norton's balls a squeeze every now and again and smile up at him with a devilish gleam in her wild green eyes. Eventually she stopped, gave her hair a toss, then lay back on the bed with her head on the pillows. Les spied the little pine cone sticking out and was thinking of giving it a quick munch. Then figured after eight hours in a hot greasy kitchen, the croissant wouldn't quite be fresh from the patisserie. Instead, he rolled the condom down over Mr Wobbly, got between Janet's long lean legs and pushed.

Les had no trouble getting Mr Wobbly inside Janet and soon started pumping and banging away with great gusto. The only problem was, the minute Les got a rhythm going, the bed would take off against the nearest wall, stop, then take off again, finishing against either another wall, the window, or the set of drawers.

'Shit! What's happening with the ceiling?' said Janet.

'Why? Does it need painting?' asked Les.

'No. It needs nailing down. Christ! This is like hevving sexxx in a dodgem car.'

'Yes. It's certainly a wild old ride,' agreed Les.

Nevertheless, Janet soon got used to her disorientation and squealed with delight, kicking her long legs up in the air, tongue kissing Les and nibbling on his neck with her buck teeth. Les pounded away, giving it all he had before he heard Janet howl and get her rocks off beneath him. Then Norton figured it was his turn. He got his arms under Janet's legs, lifted them up over her head and thundered away towards the finishing line like Phar Lap coming down the straight. Janet yelled encouragement and spurred Les on. Les shut his eyes, stiffened his legs and with one last burst, groaned and emptied out, leaving Mr Wobbly a shattered man inside his little rubber raincoat. When they'd finished, the bed was back against the window. Les put a pillow under both their heads, pulled the duvet over them and put his arm around Janet.

'Well, that was a lot of fun, Janet,' smiled Les. 'You caught me a little off-guard. But I gave it my best shot.'

'It was very good, Les,' Janet smiled back. 'If ever you're up this way again, call in at the Sailing Club for another T-bone.'

'I will,' promised Les. He gave Janet a kiss on the cheek. 'You want a glass of water or something?'

'I wouldn't mind a beer.'

'Yeah. Good idea.'

Les got out of bed, dumped the condom down the toilet then came back with two cold bottles of Becks from the fridge. They sat up in bed, clinked their bottles together and both took healthy pulls. After a good belch each they settled down and enjoyed their beers.

'You know, there's something I've got to ask you, Janet,' said Les.

'Sure. What's that, Les?' she replied.

'Well. Getting you and Ruby back here tonight.

Tony was a bit sort of, I dunno, secretive. "Is everything sweet for tonight?" "Are we still on?" "What time are you going to be here?"' Les looked evenly at Janet. 'Ruby's not married, is she?'

'No,' said Janet. 'But she's got a really jealous boyfriend. Richard.'

'Oh?' said Les. 'And what's Richard do? I suppose he's a builder?'

'No. He's a chef. Does mostly catering. He's doing a big job tonight at Taree. That's why Ruby was able to get away.'

'What's he look like?'

'Tall. Long black hair. Got a trimmed black beard and wears a big gold earring. I always say he looks like a pirate,' Janet giggled.

'Shit! Ruby must fancy Tony,' said Les.

'She does. We all do,' grinned Janet. 'He's a doll. He's a cheeky bugger. But he's still a doll.'

Suddenly the bedroom door swung open, taking Les by surprise, and Tony was standing there with a towel wrapped round him holding a can of JD and Coke.

'Steelo. What the fuck do you want?' said Les.

'Not you, Ugly,' replied Tony, 'that's for fuckin sure.' He dropped the towel and crawled under the duvet alongside Janet, spilling drink on the bed.

'Hello, Janet. You gorgeous big thing,' he grinned. 'Give Tony a little kiss.'

'Tony, what do you think this is?' laughed Janet. 'Go on. Get out of here.'

'Yeah. You heard her, Steelo,' said Les. 'Piss off. Strike me hooray! This happens to be the girl I love.'

'Girl you love. Ohh don't give me the shits.' Tony placed his drink on the floor and started kissing Janet on the neck. 'Come here, Janet,' he drooled. 'You unbelievable spunk. Grrrhh.'

'Tony. You're a beast,' said Janet. 'Get away, you little devil.'

Les shook his head and got out of bed. 'Janet,' he said, climbing back into his shorts and T-shirt. 'I might leave you to work this out. He's too much of a doll for me.'

'Yeah, fuck off, Les,' laughed Tony. 'And hand the job over to a real man.'

'Tony. Stop that,' said Janet. 'And take your hand off my snetch.'

'That's not all I'd like to slip round your snetch,' said Tony, running his tongue over his lips.

Leaving the door ajar, Les left Tony and Janet to their own devices and sat down in the loungeroom with his beer to listen to the radio. The bathroom door opened and Ruby came out wearing a lacy blue bra and a pair of white knickers with blue diamonds on them.

'Hello, Ruby,' smiled Les. 'Lovely evening, isn't it?'

'Yes, it is,' replied Ruby, showing absolutely no embarrassment. 'Where's Tony?'

Les nodded to his bedroom. 'In there, trying to rape Janet.'

'That wouldn't surprise me,' said Ruby. 'Why aren't you in there protecting her honour?'

'I was. But he forced me out of the room. Janet helped him.'

'That lousy bitch,' huffed Ruby. 'She'll pay for this.'

Next thing, Janet came out of Norton's bedroom with her clothes back on, waving her hands in the air. She saw Ruby and shook her head.

'He's just as mad as ever,' laughed Janet. 'Worse. The stupid bugger.'

'I'll kill the prick,' said Ruby.

Les was staring up at Janet when Tony came out of Norton's bedroom with his towel in one hand, his drink in the other and a big grin on his face.

'Hello, gang,' he said. 'What's happening?'

'Oh, Tony. Put some bloody clothes on, will you,' said Ruby. 'You look ridiculous.'

'Yes. Get dressed, Tony,' added Janet. 'You'll catch your death of cold.'

'I won't if you warm me up,' said Tony.

Ruby pushed Tony back into his bedroom and followed him inside, while Janet went to the bathroom, leaving Les alone in the loungeroom. Les finished his beer, then Janet came out of the bathroom, went to the kitchen and took a mobile phone from her bag. Tony and Ruby came out of Tony's bedroom laughing and, fully dressed, sat down on the lounge. A moment or two later, Janet put her phone back in her bag and sat down in a lounge chair close to Les.

'I rang Andrew,' Janet said to Ruby. 'He'll be here in about five minutes.'

'Good,' yawned Ruby. 'I'm buggered.'

'Buggered?' said Tony. 'Get out. Let's kick on. There's a heap of piss left in the fridge.'

Ruby poked her finger in Tony's chest. 'Tony,' she said. 'You've had enough booze tonight for ten people. Now behave yourself.'

'Ohh, Red?' pleaded Tony.

'You heard.' Ruby squeezed Tony's nose. 'Behave yourself.'

'All right, my sweetest Rose,' said Tony, kissing Ruby on the lips.

Les leaned over to Janet. 'This Andrew, your cousin who does the security, is he a mate of Richard's?'

Janet nodded. 'They're both in the surf club. In the boat crew.'

Les nodded back. 'Fair enough.'

The radio had just finished playing the Hoodoo Gurus' 'Like Wow — Wipeout' when a car horn tooted out the front.

'This'll be Andrew,' said Janet.

Janet and Ruby got to their feet and straightened themselves up. Les and Tony stood up. Les put his arms around Janet.

'Well, Janet,' Les smiled warmly. 'What can I say? If ever I'm up this way again, I'll make sure I see you.'

'Yes. You'll always find me at the club. Tony's got my mobile phone number.'

'Good.'

Les gave Janet a goodnight kiss. Tony did the same with Ruby. Then the girls picked up their bags and shuffled towards the door.

'Hang on,' insisted Tony. 'I'll walk you down to the car.'

'There's really no need to,' said Ruby.

'We'll be all right,' added Janet. 'Christ! It's only down the bottom of the stairs.'

Tony was adamant. 'No. I'll walk you down. I'm a gentleman.'

'Oh. I can vouch for that,' said Les.

Tony walked out the door with the two girls and ushered them down the stairs while Les stepped out onto the balcony. Parked below was a dark blue Ford Focus hatchback. The driver's door was open and standing beside the car looking up was a tall man in a black jacket and trousers. He had close-cropped curly hair and even from the balcony Les noticed a resemblance between him and Janet. The man caught Norton's eye before Tony appeared out front with the girls. The man got back behind the wheel, Tony opened the door and Ruby sat in the front while Janet piled in the back. The car turned around and drove out into the street, Les stepped inside and shortly after, Tony returned, closing the door behind him.

'Well, what do you reckon, Ugly?' he grinned. 'Did I tell you we'd be in for some fun and games tonight or what?'

'Yes. I have to give it to you, Steelo,' replied Les. 'When it comes to sheilas, you're definitely Charlie Charm Pot.'

'I have my moments,' said Tony. 'Anyway. Get fucked, Les, I'm going to clean my teeth and go to bed. I'm rooted.'

'Yeah. So am I,' yawned Les. 'What do you want to do for breakfast? I found a nice little café in the village.'

'Ohh, see what happens when we surface in the morning,' Tony yawned back.

'Righto.'

Tony went to the bathroom. Les had a drink of mineral water then followed Tony. When Les had finished, he switched off the lights and the ghetto blaster, got down to his T-shirt and jox and climbed into bed, throwing his leg across where Tony had spilled his drink.

'Fuck you, Steelo!' Les cursed.

Les got out of bed, found his towel in the darkness and placed it over the wet part of the sheet. Fair dinkum, scowled Norton, climbing back under the duvet and scrunching his head into the pillows. The things a man has to put up with when he's trying to have a holiday. The aroma of Janet's body oil lingered on the pillows and it smelled lovely. Les took a few deep breaths in through his nose, smiled, then took a couple more. It wasn't long and he was out like a light.

Les had a good sleep-in the next morning. The sun was well and truly up when he finally blinked his eyes open and peered out the bedroom window to discover a bright sunny day with a few clouds drifting across the sky and the wind blowing softly towards the ocean. The previous night's festivities suddenly filled Norton's mind and he gingerly got out of bed and stepped into the loungeroom. Crumpled corn chip packets, glasses and empty bottles were scattered everywhere. Tony's door was slightly ajar and from inside his bedroom came the sound of light snoring. Les left Tony in peace and, nursing a rude headache, padded to the bathroom.

Cleaning his teeth, Les was pleased to see Janet's buck teeth hadn't left any love bites when she was gnawing on his neck. After dropping two Panadeine capsules he finished in the bathroom, then stepped into the kitchen.

Ahh yes, smiled Norton, opening the fridge. Nothing like a hearty breakfast to get a man going first thing in the morning. Taking a fork, Les speared two slices of grilled eggplant and washed them down with a cup of hot tap water. And now, gritted Les, as he collected his training gear from the back verandah, while I'm still filthy on myself, I'll take my hangover for a run and have a swim. Stoically, Les climbed into his training gear and thongs and left for Blueys Beach. Shit! he lamented, as he stopped at the open air shower to get a mouthful of water and wipe his sunglasses, what I wouldn't give for a good cup of coffee right now.

Apart from a handful of surfers enjoying the clean swells, two couples lying on the sand and the same seagulls at the water's edge, Les had the beach to himself again. He returned the greetings of a young couple stretched out comfortably on their banana chairs near the wet sand, left his towel and thongs close by and took off.

Not feeling the hairy chest, Les cut the run back to six laps. The Panadeine capsules hit in after two, so the last four laps were almost bearable. The water when he'd finished, however, was glorious. Les wallowed around for a while, duck diving and letting the waves break over his face, then walked up and had a cold shower. Back at the flat, Tony was up and about. He'd cleaned up the mess and was standing in the kitchen wearing his grey shorts and a white T-shirt, drinking a glass of mineral water with ice and a slice of lemon.

'Les, you've been for a run,' he smiled. 'You're a fuckin tiger. How was it?'

'Sort of all right, Steelo,' replied Les. 'The water was good though.'

'Hey. I knocked off a couple of your Panadeine tablets. I had to, mate.'

'That's okay,' smiled Les. 'I needed some myself.' Les hung his training gear and towel out on the verandah then walked back into the kitchen in his Speedos and poured himself a large glass of water.

'Hey, what about last night,' said Tony. 'Christ! Didn't we put away some piss.'

'Ohh, don't talk to me about last night, Steelo,' said Les, downing one glass of water and pouring another. 'You're a depraved fuckin animal. I'm in there talking sweet nothings with Janet, and you kick the door open, barge in and try to rape her in front of me. You're fuckin good.'

'Ohh, fuck off, Les,' said Tony. 'Me and Janet the Gannet have been friends for years.'

'Yeah? That's not what Ruby said. She wanted to call the police, only I talked her out of it.'

'Les. Get fucked. You're a fuckin imposter.'

'All right,' shrugged Les. 'So what are we doing for breakfast?' He looked at his watch. 'Christ! It's almost lunchtime.'

'All right. What about that café you found?'

'Okay. We'll go there. I'll shout.'

'No!' Tony was adamant. 'I'll pay. I didn't come here to bludge off you. Get fucked.'

'Tony,' winked Les, 'thanks to you, I had a pretty good time last night. Let me shout.'

'All right,' shrugged Tony. 'If you want to pay, pay. Fuck you.'

'Thanks, Steelo.'

Les changed into his blue shorts and a maroon T-shirt with LORNE on the front, gave his hair a quick tidy, then he and Tony walked down to the car and drove into the village.

Several cars were parked outside the shops and there was a smattering of punters strolling about in the sun when Les pulled up out the front of Fifty-Fifty. Not wasting any time, Les walked straight into the café and up to the smiling young lady wearing a black T-shirt standing behind the counter. He ordered bacon and scrambled eggs on Turkish with mushrooms, a double shot latte and a bottle of sparkling mineral water. Tony ordered the same, except for a flat white and a bowl of muesli. They found a table out front, Les went and got the papers, then with Norton facing the parking area and the road behind, they settled back comfortably and waited for their food.

The coffee came first and it had life-saving properties. Les knocked his over smartly and ordered another when the food arrived. There was plenty on the plates and it was all cooked to perfection.

'Strike me! They sure give you enough,' said Les.

'Don't worry, Les,' replied Tony. 'I've seen you eat. You'll knock that over in a New York minute and start banging on the table for more.'

Les looked straight down his nose at Tony. 'Jesus you're a peasant at times, Steelo,' he sniffed. 'You really are.'

'Get fucked, Les, and stop uttering shit. You're a big enough goose as it is.'

Both ravenously hungry, they ripped in and although Tony also had a bowl of muesli, it was a dead heat who finished first. Les was going through the sports section and washing down the remaining toast with his second coffee when he noticed a familiar blue hatchback drive past. It slowed down near the bottle shop, made a U-turn, then came back and drove slowly through the parking area with the windows down. Les absently turned a page and from behind his sunglasses noticed Janet's cousin at the wheel and a tall bloke with a black ponytail seated on the passenger side. Both men were wearing old football guernseys with the sleeves hacked off and in the bright autumn sun, a glint of gold reflected from the ear of the man alongside the driver. Well, mused Les, slowly turning another page. That's Andrew from last night. And I'd say the sour-faced bloke with him is Richard the jealous boyfriend. Very casually, Les watched as the two men took a good look before the hatchback left the parking area and drove off towards Elizabeth Beach. I won't say anything to Steelo for the time being, thought Les. But I'll definitely warn him about Sourpuss before I go.

'Shit! I'm rooted after that,' said Tony, folding his newspaper.

'Yeah. Me too,' said Les.

Tony reached for his pocket. 'You sure you don't want some money?'

Les shook his head. 'No. You're right, mate. I'll put it on the plastic fantastic.'

'Okay. Well thanks for that, Les. I'm going to get a bar of chocolate.'

'If you want, you can shout me a Cherry Ripe and a Peanut Slab while you're there.'

'No worries. I'll see you back at the car.'

Les was seated in the Berlina when Tony returned. He handed Les his chocolates and they drove back to the flat.

'So what are you going to do now, Steelo?' Les asked when they walked in the door.

'Not much,' replied Tony, going to the kitchen and pouring a glass of mineral water. 'Kick back. Muck around on the laptop. Hey, I wouldn't mind a couple more of your Panadeine, if it's okay. I've still got a bit of a headache.'

'Yeah. Mine seems to have kicked in again too,' said Les.

'So what are you going to do?' asked Tony, stepping into the bathroom to get the Panadeine.

'After all that food, just take it easy,' replied Les. 'Probably lie down and have a read.'

'What are you reading?' Tony called out.

'*AK-47, the Story of the People's Gun*, by Michael Hodges.'

'Read it,' enthused Tony, walking back into the lounge. 'Isn't it a fuckin good book.'

'Reckon,' agreed Les. 'What about poor old General Kalashnikov who invented the thing. They've sold millions round the world, and he never got a razoo.'

'No. They wouldn't even let him put the name on a brand of vodka. Yet Stoner, the Yank who invented the M-16, made squillions. And it isn't anywhere near as good a weapon.'

Les went to his room and came back with his wedding invitation. 'Hey, Steelo,' he asked. 'How come the wedding's so late in the afternoon?'

'The sun will be going down on Wallis Lake. And it'll make for great photos,' replied Tony.

'Fair enough,' nodded Les. 'And where, and what's, this — Green Cathedral?'

'It's an open-air church in a rainforest a few clicks past the Sailing Club. Wait till you see it. It's the grouse.'

'Sounds good.'

Les left Tony to his laptop then went to the bathroom and took a couple more Panadeine. He propped the pillows up behind his head, lay down on the bed with his book and his Peanut Slab and started munching and reading.

Norton's house in Bondi was reasonably quiet for the city. But the warm, sunny flat at Blueys Beach was quieter and the bed when it wasn't rolling around was extremely comfortable. Besides that, just the thought of being away from Sydney gave everything a feeling of peace and relaxation. Les got to a part in his book where American soldiers in Vietnam, cursing their constantly jamming M-16s, started picking up the Viet Cong's more reliable AK-47s. Other American soldiers would hear the AK-47's distinct sound coming from the jungle, think it was Charlie, and start shooting their fellow soldiers. This brought much joy and laughter to the beleaguered Vietnamese and even had Les smiling, when the quietness and the Panadeine got to him. Eventually his eyes started to flicker and he dozed off.

'Hey, Les. Come on. We'd better make a move.'

'Huh?' Les blinked his eyes open to find Tony with a towel round him shaking the end of the bed. 'Shit. What time is it?'

'Time to get going, you big goose.'

Les sat up on the bed. 'Fuck. I dozed off. It's so bloody peaceful up here.'

'Yeah. So did I,' smiled Tony. 'It's not hard.'

'All right,' said Les, 'I'll jump under the shower.'

Les showered and shaved and helped himself to some of Tony's Fahrenheit, then changed into a pair of jeans and a fresh white T-shirt with a blue check shirt hanging out over the top. Tony was waiting in the lounge wearing jeans and a grey T-shirt with a black diagonal-striped shirt hanging out over the top.

'I say, Steelo,' grinned Les. 'We haven't brushed up too bad for a couple of mugs from the Eastern Suburbs.'

'No. You look wonderful, Leslie,' smiled Tony.

'Leslie?' Norton's eyes narrowed. 'By Jesus! Them's fighting words, Steelo.'

'Get fucked, Les,' said Tony. 'And just get me to the church on time.'

Les picked up his Canon Power Shot, Tony placed his Canon EOS ID Mk3 carefully in his carrybag, then locked the door and followed Les down to the Berlina before they drove off towards Wallis Lake.

Cars were parked along either side of the road and the last of the guests were arriving when Les did a U-turn and pulled up opposite the wedding venue. They got out of the car and Les recognised one or two of Steve's casually dressed mates and their girls from the night before, amidst several older couples of Slavic appearance getting out of their cars wearing conservative suits and dresses. Les and Tony exchanged greetings with Steve's friends, then crossed the road to a shaded path leading into a lush rainforest thick with ferns.

The path meandered through tall trees and native bushes to an open-air church consisting of two rows of roughly hewn wooden pews either side of an aisle of white sand leading to a stone pulpit. Behind the pulpit was the lake where huge old logs washed up on the shore rested in the quiet shade of the surrounding trees. The water was dead calm and the sun setting behind the distant hills had turned the lake into a seemingly endless expanse of shimmering gold.

'Shit. You weren't wrong about taking good photos,' said Les. 'How cool's this?'

'What did I tell you,' smiled Tony. 'Isn't it something else?'

The congregation had split into two camps seated on either side of the aisle, with the impassive family members on the right dressed in dark blue suits and dark blue dresses, while the impassive family members on the left were wearing brown suits and brown dresses. Steve's friends and their kids were towards the back and Les noticed that apart from Steve's friends smiling amongst themselves and the children playing, there wasn't a great deal of laughter in the air for such a joyous occasion. Standing to the left of the pulpit and holding flowers were the four bridesmaids dressed in beige dresses with matching shoes. Lined up to the right of the pulpit were Steve, Cunzdrug and another two of Steve's mates, all wearing immaculately ironed white shirts with small garlands of flowers pinned to the front, hanging out over green trousers and white leather thongs. Standing casually in the lush ambience of the Green Cathedral, with Cat Power crooning 'Sea of Love' in the background, their crisp informality blended perfectly with the occasion.

'Shit,' said Les. 'Check out Deadline and his mates. I hope Saretta isn't going to show up wearing white thongs.'

'Well, you know the old joke,' replied Tony. 'How do you tell the bride at an Australian wedding?'

'Yeah,' smiled Les. He indicated the soberly dressed members of the congregation seated stiffly along the pews. 'So who's who at the zoo?'

'Deadline's family are the ones in brown. And Saretta's are the ones in blue. One thing for sure, Les, I don't think any of them are into stand-up comedy.'

'No. You're not wrong.' Les pointed to several empty pews at the rear. 'Anyway. What do you reckon, Steelo? We may as well prop here.'

'Yeah, this'll do.' Tony placed his camera bag on the nearest pew and unzipped it. 'I'm going to get some photos while the light's still good.'

'I might join you,' replied Les.

Cameras in hand, they walked down the aisle and up to Steve and his friends. After shaking hands and wishing them all the best, Les and Tony started taking photos. Les got all the happy snaps he needed for the time being. Tony the professional kept clicking away from all angles till he rejoined Les sitting at the end of the pews.

'How did you go, Steelo?' Les asked. 'Get some good shots?'

'Are you kidding?' replied Tony. 'Did you see the water on the lake? You couldn't go wrong.'

'I know. Check this out.' Les scrolled the screen on his digital camera and showed Tony some shots he'd fluked.

'Holy fuck,' said Tony. 'I'm going to have to watch you, Norton. Or you'll end up doing me out of a job.'

Along with the rest of the congregation, Les and Tony sat patiently waiting for the ceremony to start. The celebrant, a dark-haired woman in a smart grey dress suit, appeared by the pulpit with a roving mike and Les was surreptitiously checking out a couple of Saretta's girlfriends seated amongst the crowd when something made him turn around. Saretta came walking down the path through the rainforest on her father's arm. Les nudged Tony, who also turned around and they both gave a double blink.

Wearing a white off-the-shoulder gown that hugged her body like paint, Saretta looked drop dead gorgeous. A half-veil discreetly covered her face and her hair was styled on top of her head and ringed with tiny flowers. She was carrying a bunch of flowers and Saretta didn't just walk into the ceremony, she entered. It was her day and she knew it. And her father, a tall, jowly man with thick dark hair wearing a blue suit, knew it too as he proudly escorted his daughter down the aisle. The congregation fell silent and Les turned to Tony after Saretta and her father went past.

'Shit! Did you see that?' said Les.

'She looks like a million fuckin dollars,' replied Tony.

Saretta walked up to the front of the church and gave Steve a smile that buckled his knees and made the groomsmen shuffle around speechless. Then the celebrant stepped up to the pulpit with the roving mike.

'Ladies and gentlemen,' the celebrant began, 'we are gathered here on this joyous occasion to …'

From there the ceremony went like clockwork. Saretta gave a little speech about how she first met Steve before falling in love with him and how he warmed up her life. Steve then took the mike and looked at Saretta.

'Yeah. Well, it's good you love me, Saretta,' he said. 'Because I really, really like you a lot too, you know.'

'That's our boy, Deadline,' smiled Tony.

Les gave a little shake of his head. 'Yeah. You can't help but like him.'

Steve finished the rest of his speech, then he and Saretta exchanged gold rings. The celebrant pronounced them man and wife and as G. Love softly singing 'I Love You' drifted from the speakers, she told Steve he could now kiss the bride. Steve kissed his beautiful bride, the kids ran up and hugged their legs and it was all over.

'Oh shit!' swallowed Les. 'Why did they have to pick this song? I think I'm gonna cry.'

'Yeah. Me too,' sniffed Tony.

'This is bloody awful.'

'Yeah,' agreed Tony. 'If word gets around you were seen blubbering at a wedding, your reputation round the Cross'll be ratshit.'

'I know,' said Les. 'Promise you won't tell anybody, Tony.'

Tony suddenly raised his camera and whipped off a close-up of Norton's distraught face. 'I'll think about it,' he grinned.

'You two-faced rotten cunt, Steelo,' cursed Les.

'Get fucked, Les,' said Tony.

All the congregation now wanted to get a photo taken with the happy couple and somewhere between Saretta's beauty and the loveliness of the Green Cathedral the earlier animosity between the two families seemed to have momentarily disappeared. After a while, Les handed Tony his camera and got a couple of photos taken standing between Steve and Saretta. Tony got Les to do the same with his camera, then they went back to their seats and watched absently as everybody began to drift off around them. Before Les and Tony knew it, they were the only ones left, still seated, staring at the sun going down over the lake.

'Well I suppose we'd better get going, Les,' said Tony. 'I wouldn't mind a few drinks back at the flat before we hit the reception.'

'Righto,' nodded Les. 'It's just that it's so nice here. I don't want to leave.'

'Yeah. I know what you mean,' agreed Tony.

Les turned to Tony. 'Another couple of minutes won't hurt?'

'No. Not in the least.'

The sun finally went down behind the hills ringing the lake and Les and Tony walked back to the car.

Seeing as they'd given their booze supply a decent nudge the night before, Les stopped at the bottle shop on the way home and bought another bottle of Jack Daniel's and more mineral water, while Tony bought a six-pack of JD and Coke.

Back at the flat, Tony beat Les to the bathroom then they made themselves comfortable in the loungeroom and got into the drink while they talked about the wedding and blokey things as Norton's ghetto blaster pumped out a steady stream of old rock 'n roll favourites in the background.

'So where's the reception again, Steelo?' asked Les.

Tony nodded behind the flats. 'About half a click down the road overlooking the beach. They've rented a big place especially for the occasion.'

'Beautiful,' smiled Les, raising his drink 'We can walk down with a travelling delicious.'

Tony raised his can of JD and Coke. 'We sure can, dude.'

'And what's with the "no presents" on the invitation? Give a donation instead?'

'Yeah. Deadline reckons it's better if everyone throws in a few bucks, rather than have him finish up with twenty electric toasters and a hundred tea towels.'

'Good idea,' said Les. 'Okay. I'm in for a hundred.'

'Me too,' smiled Tony.

Les handed Tony two fifties, Tony got a distinctive blue envelope from his room and placed their money inside along with a sheet of paper signed by both of them wishing Steve and Saretta all the best. Tony then sealed the envelope and put it in the back pocket of his jeans.

'Did Deadline tell you I'm heading north tomorrow? So I won't be able to drive you back to Sydney,' said Les.

'Yeah. No problems,' replied Tony. 'I can get a lift home with Cunzdrug and Errol.'

'Beauty.'

'So where are you going?' asked Tony.

'Lennox Head,' lied Les. 'To see a bloke I used to play football with. Burt Zane.'

'I know Burt,' said Tony. 'He was a good second rower. Till he fucked his knee up.'

'Mate. He could tackle. I know that,' smiled Les.

They threw down a few more drinks. Tony bonked a few girls and photographed several young models, while Les scored a couple of tries under the posts and sorted out the odd mug with Billy Dunne. Finally Tony looked at his watch.

'We may as well get going,' he said. 'Deadline and the boys'll be wondering where we are.'

'Yeah. Good idea,' agreed Les. 'Let's blast off.'

Along with the bottle of Jack Daniel's, Tony placed his six-pack of JD and Coke into a plastic shopping bag, then, carrying what they were drinking, Les and Tony left the flat and headed for the wedding reception.

The venue was a huge wooden house, built with Blueys Beach at the rear. A double garage faced the street and on the right a set of stairs lined with candles led up to the front door. Les and Tony followed the candles and stepped through into a large open deck area, scattered with outdoor furniture. Right off the front door was a bathroom and toilet and next to that a sizeable loungeroom with a set of stairs running up to the next floor. The loungeroom faced a bar on the left side of the house where two girls were pouring beers and handing out glasses of wine, and next to the bar was an open kitchen staffed by people in black or white uniforms passing out food or working at the hot plates. The house finished at a wide sundeck built above a backyard full of trees that commanded a beautiful view of Blueys Beach shining in the moonlight. The reception was crowded and two girls in white uniforms were easing their way through the guests with trays of food. Steve was joking with two mates near the loungeroom while Saretta was seated inside on a black leather lounge with her father and two bridesmaids. Cruisy lounge music was playing in the background, the children had been all put to bed and Steve's friends were getting into the occasion. Around them, in a sea of alcohol, the two families in brown and blue were doing their best to forget past differences and straining to enjoy themselves as best they could.

'Well, isn't this nice, Steelo,' said Les, helping himself to a chicken kebab going past on a tray. 'A nice big place full of nice big people.'

'Yeah. And all nice and pissed,' said Tony, grabbing two spring rolls from another passing tray.

A short wall ran between the deck and the bar and Les pointed to an empty table in the corner. 'Why don't we place our drinks on that table? I'll get some ice and soda water. Then we might mingle.'

'Righto,' nodded Tony.

Tony placed the plastic bag on a white outdoor table while Les stepped round to the bar and got two glasses of ice and a bottle of soda water. While he was waiting, Les turned to the open kitchen and noticed a tall man in a black T-shirt morosely turning kebabs on a hot plate. He had a neatly trimmed beard and long black hair pinned back in a ponytail that exposed a thick gold earring. Well, look who's on the job, mused Les. Richard the jealous boyfriend. And he doesn't look any happier than he did this morning. I'm not sure where his head's at, but I think it might be best if I try and keep Steelo away from him till we leave. Les got his ice and soda water and walked back to the table.

'Well done, Les,' said Tony, taking a glass of ice and pouring his can of JD and Coke into it. 'I might even add a bit of your Jack Daniel's.'

'Help yourself.' Les made himself a delicious and watched as Tony topped up his glass with bourbon.

'Ohh, yeah,' said Tony, smacking his lips. 'That certainly hits the spot.'

'It certainly does,' agreed Les.

'I'll tell you what,' said Tony. 'Those spring rolls were the grouse. I'm going down to get some more.'

'Get some more?' said Les. 'Where?'

'Where?' Tony nodded past the bar. 'Where they're cooking them, you big goose. Where do you think?'

'Let me,' smiled Les. 'I'll get them.'

'No. I'll get them,' said Tony, placing his drink on the table. 'What do you think I am? A fuckin cripple? Besides, I want to give Deadline his envelope.'

'Okay. You're the boss,' replied Les. 'I'll wait here.'

Stepping away from the table, Les watched Tony walk up to Steve and hand him the blue envelope.

Steve shook Tony's hand, then turned around, waved and smiled a thank you to Les. Les smiled back and raised his glass. After a moment or two Tony left Steve with his mates and walked down to the kitchen.

A couple of people moved away and Tony stepped up to a skinny blonde girl at the counter wearing a white uniform. They exchanged smiles then the girl picked up two paper plates and stepped across to Richard. Richard placed a serving of spring rolls and kebabs on the plates before absently turning around towards the counter. The second Richard saw Tony, he stiffened and his eyes started spinning around in his head like Tibetan prayer wheels. The blonde girl handed Tony the plates and Tony eased his way towards the deck area totally oblivious to the filthy looks he was getting from the kitchen. Keeping the guests between himself and the other end of the house, edging forward, Les watched Richard pick up a spatula and, still staring daggers at Tony, stab angrily at the food on the hot plates. Sipping his bourbon, Les stepped back to their table.

'Here you go, Ugly,' said Tony, placing the paper plates on the table. 'Help yourself.'

'Thanks, Steelo. You're a legend.' Les picked up a kebab and chewed a piece off. 'So what did Deadline have to say?'

'Ohh, he was rapt,' replied Tony. 'He's coming over in a minute to have a drink with us.'

'Good.' Les finished his kebab and picked up his drink. 'Hey, Tony,' he said. 'I think there's something I should tell you.'

Tony finished his JD and Coke and put his glass down. 'Tell me when I get back from the brascoe. I got to have a snakes.'

'All right,' nodded Les.

Tony walked across to the toilet and in full view of Richard stood outside and waited for the person inside to finish. Still keeping himself inconspicuous, Les edged up to the bar and pensively watched Richard glaring like a madman at Tony. A stocky woman in a blue dress stepped out of the toilet and Tony went inside. He'd no sooner closed the door when Janet's cousin Andrew walked in the front door wearing his blue uniform. He spotted Richard looking towards the toilet, gave him a wave and started walking down to the kitchen, not seeing Les near the bar. Hello, Richard's mate's here, noticed Les. I wonder what he wants? Probably a free feed, I would imagine.

Andrew walked up to the counter and Richard immediately left what was on the hot plates and got into an animated discussion with his friend.

Richard was pointing angrily towards the toilet when the door opened and Tony came out wiping his hands, before walking across to the table to get a fresh drink. This was enough for Richard. He tore off his apron, flung it on the counter and stormed up through the guests to Tony. Tony was about to take a sip of his JD and Coke and join Les when Richard loomed up in front of him and pushed him in the chest, spilling Tony's drink over his shirt.

'What the …?' said Tony, going backwards.

'Did you have a good time last night?' demanded Richard.

Tony gave Richard a bewildered once-up-and-down. 'What are you talking about, you goose?'

'Ruby. The girl you were with last night. That's my fuckin girlfriend.'

'She is?'

'Yeah. So what have you got to say about it?'

Tony thought for a second. 'Nothing really,' he replied. 'Except you're a lucky man. Because she's an unbelievable fuck. And she could suck paint off the Harbour Bridge.'

The tall rangy cook immediately exploded. 'Aaarrgghh!'

Seething with rage, Richard brought his right arm back and punched Tony hard in the face, sending Tony into a couple behind him dressed in brown. Stunned, and with blood pouring from his nose, Tony did his best to stay on his feet when Richard grabbed him with his left hand and started pummelling Tony's head with his right. Tony was having absolutely no luck at all, so reluctantly Les decided he'd better step in before Steelo finished up looking like topside mince. Putting his drink down, Les moved quickly through the guests and pulled Richard off Tony.

'Righto, tough guy. You've proved your point,' said Les. 'He's had enough. Leave him alone.'

'Who the fuck are you?' snarled Richard.

'A friend of his. Now piss off. Go on, you've had your fun.'

'What? Fuck you.'

Richard drew back to head-butt Les. Les brought his hand up to his forehead and all Richard's big bony head collected was the heel of Norton's fist. Les slammed his left knee into Richard's groin and as he doubled up with pain, grabbed him by the front of his black T-shirt and smashed two short rights into Richard's face, splitting his eye open and mashing up his mouth. Richard started to sink so Les brought his right knee up into his face and Richard's nose turned into a squashed blob of bone and gristle resting under one eye. Les dropped Richard on the floor and turned just in time to see Andrew knocking people's drinks over as he charged through the guests to get at Norton. Les stepped back a little and Andrew ran straight into a hideous left hook that tore his mouth open, knocked out all his front teeth and buckled his knees. Blood bubbling down his chin, Andrew's eyes glazed over and he was about to join his teeth rattling around on the floor when Les bent down, hooked his right arm under Andrew's crotch, got hold of his jacket with his left arm, then stood up and with a quick shoulder wheel easily flipped Andrew back amongst the bemused guests standing round the bar. The tall security guard's left arm landed on the bar as he came down, knocking over a tray of beers, and his right arm hit a woman in a brown dress across the ears, knocking her hat off and spilling her drink over her.

And that was it. The catalyst the party had been waiting for. Everybody wearing blue figured somebody wearing brown had spilled their drink over them, and everybody wearing brown thought exactly the reverse. Within seconds, the reception erupted into a huge, rolling blood feud, and if somebody in blue couldn't find somebody in brown to punch or kick and if somebody in brown couldn't find someone in blue to kick and punch, they turned on the nearest waxhead.

Ducking under a bar stool flying past, Les picked Tony up from where he was sitting on his rump on the floor and placed him on a chair at their table. The blood had stopped flowing freely from Tony's nose and was now just a steady trickle.

'Are you all right, Steelo?' asked Les, as a flying bottle smashed against the wall behind their table.

'Ohh, what the fuck happened?' groaned Tony, staring at the blood all over the front of his shirt.

'You started a fight,' answered Les. 'And you got sorted out for your trouble. You idiot.'

'I started a fight?'

'Yeah,' nodded Les. 'Have a look around you. This is all your fault. You're a madman.'

Tony looked up in horror. 'Oh shit!'

People were going through windows, getting thrown over the bar or tossed off the balcony. Saretta's father had two men wearing brown in headlocks and was banging their heads together. Saretta, her hair all over the place and a huge rip in her wedding dress, was sitting on some woman in brown's stomach, smashing a high heel into the woman's face, while the woman was reaching up, trying to scratch Saretta's eyes out. Near the bar, a man in blue fighting a man in brown was going all right till a woman in a smart brown dress smashed a champagne bottle over the man in blue's head, knocking him cold. Cunzdrug, his blond hair a bigger mess than ever and his crisp white shirt covered in blood and hanging off his back in tatters, was standing in the lounge fighting a solid man in blue and giving quite a good account of himself when another man in blue whacked him across the kidneys with a bar stool. Cunzdrug went down and both men started kicking him till two of the groomsmen, their white shirts torn to shreds, jumped in and saved him.

'Shit. You know what we forgot, Steelo?' said Les.

'What?' said Tony.

'Our cameras,' replied Les. 'How good's this?'

'Ohh, get fucked, Les.'

Another bottle smashed into the wall behind them and a plastic chair came skidding across the floor and cannoned into their table when Steve lurched out of the loungeroom holding a man in brown in a headlock and punching the man in the face. His shirt torn off his back and huge rips in his green trousers, Steve was going all right till the man in brown got hold of one of Steve's legs and flipped him over, turning their fight into a biting, gouging wrestling match on the beer and blood sodden floor.

'Come on, Steelo,' said Les. 'I think it's time you and I made a discreet exit.'

'You're not fuckin wrong,' cursed Tony, spitting a gob of blood onto the floor.

Les bundled the last of their booze back into the plastic bag, along with the remaining kebabs and spring rolls. He was about to help Tony up when he noticed a familiar patch of blue amongst the mess on the floor.

'Hey, wait here a sec, Steelo,' said Les.

Les was about to go over and pick up the envelope when a man in a torn brown suit stood on it and shaped up looking for someone to fight. Les stepped over, tapped the bloke on the shoulder and when he turned around, belted him with a crisp right uppercut. The man dropped to the floor, Les picked up the envelope, shoved it in his jeans and went back to Tony.

'You right, Steelo?' asked Les, picking up the plastic bag.

Tony rose slowly to his feet. 'Yeah. Let's get going. This is totally fucked.'

With no sign of any let-up in the fighting and people even at each other's throats in the bathroom,

Les and Tony made their way to the front door and took the stairs down to the street.

Tony was unsteady on his feet and very quiet as they made the slow journey home. Les, on the other hand, was more upbeat. He took a hit straight from the bottle of Jack Daniel's, capped it and put the bottle back in the bag.

'So, what made you want to start a fight back there, Steelo?' Les asked, taking the bourbon's bite through gritted teeth.

'Start a fight?' replied Tony. 'Fuck off, will you. I was just standing there and that big hillbilly ran up and punched me in the fuckin head.'

'Yeah? Come on, Steelo. There's got to be more to it than that.'

'Oh, he rambled on about something about Ruby being his girlfriend or some bloody thing.'

'So what did you say to him?' asked Les.

'Nothing,' lied Tony. 'I just said I didn't know. Sorry.'

'But you did know Ruby had a boyfriend,' said Les.

'Well ... yeah,' replied Tony. 'But I didn't know he was a full-on bad news fuckin imbecile.'

'Be nice if he turned on me as well,' said Les. 'I could be walking around smelling the roses through a broken nose too.'

'Ohh, fuckin bullshit, Les.'

Les shook his head. 'I don't know, Steelo. I'm not sure I can trust you any more. I think you're a crazy drunk, a lecher and a liar.'

'Get fucked, Les,' said Tony. 'You don't know what you're talking about.'

Les and Tony were almost at San Remo when the first police car came howling round the corner, followed by an ambulance. They watched another police car go screaming past, then crossed the road and walked upstairs into the flat.

Once inside, Les turned on the lights, closed the door and placed the plastic bag in the kitchen. He took out the booze, then put the kebabs and spring rolls on a plate. Tony poured himself a glass of water and flopped down on the lounge.

'You want a kebab, Steelo?' asked Les, indicating the plate.

'Do I want a kebab?' sputtered Tony. 'Have a look at my fuckin mouth. I'm lucky I got any teeth left.'

'I can cut one up for you,' suggested Les. 'Like they do for the old people in the nursing homes.'

'Ohh get fucked will you, Les,' replied Tony. 'You're a fuckin goose.'

'All right. I'm only trying to help.' Les nodded to the bathroom. 'Why don't you go and have a shower,

Steelo, and wash all the blood off you. You look like you've been in a car wreck.'

'Yeah,' Tony nodded glumly. 'I might just do that.'

'Hey. Before you go.'

'What?'

Les picked up his camera and aimed it at Tony. 'Come on. Give us a smile, mate.'

'Ohh, fuck off, Les.'

Les clicked off two close-ups. 'And one more for safety,' he grinned.

'Fuck you, Norton,' cursed Tony.

The flash went off and Norton's grin widened. 'Thanks, Steelo.'

Tony stripped off and stepped pitiably into the bathroom. Les ate a kebab and a spring roll, washed them down with a little mineral water then made himself a delicious. Pleased he hadn't torn anything during the brawl, he changed into his shorts and LORNE T-shirt and settled on a chair in the loungeroom debating whether to watch TV or listen to the radio. Les chose the radio. Queen were bopping 'Fat Bottomed Girls' when Tony came out of the shower with a towel wrapped around him. All the blood was gone, but his nose and lips were swollen, he had a lot of bark missing and one eye was starting to close.

'How do you feel now, mate?' asked Les.

'Up to shit,' replied Tony. 'That fuckin big idiot. Hey, what happened to him anyway?'

'I don't know,' replied Les. 'One minute he was standing there, punching into you. The next thing, he was lying on the floor unconscious.'

'Was that you?'

'I don't know,' shrugged Les. 'Maybe.'

'Good on you, mate,' smiled Tony. 'Hey. I helped myself to some more of your Panadeine capsules. I had to.'

'That's all right, mate,' said Les. 'If I was in your condition, I'd be howling for morphine.'

'You haven't got any, have you? I don't do drugs. But tonight I'm willing to make an exception.'

Les shook his head. 'So what are you going to do now, man of steel?'

'What am I going to do? What do you think I'm going to fuckin do,' answered Tony. 'I'm going to bed. I'm fucked.'

'I thought you might like to call Ruby. Get her and Janet round here for a few drinks. There's still plenty of piss in the fridge.'

'Yeah, terrific. All right, Les. I'll see you in the morning.'

'Okay, mate. The radio's not too loud, is it?'

'No.' Tony shook his head before he disappeared into his bedroom and closed the door. 'What a fuckin night. I can't fuckin believe it.'

Les eased back with his delicious, closed his eyes and listened to the radio. It was nice and relaxing in the flat and soon Les found himself quietly chuckling about the reception, particularly the blue envelope. Picking it up was okay. Keeping it wasn't. But what Deadline didn't know wouldn't hurt him and if somebody else hadn't picked it up, it would only have got swept out with the rubbish. Les was thinking he might leave Tony's hundred somewhere in his room where he'd find it, when there was a knock on the door. Shit, frowned Les, I wonder who this is? Norton walked over and opened the door to find Janet standing there, wearing a pair of jeans and a floppy white THREDBO T-shirt.

'Janet?'

'Les. Shit. What happened at the reception? One of my girlfriends was working there. She rang me and said it turned into a huge fight. The police came and everything.'

'They sure did,' replied Les. 'Come inside and I'll tell you all about it.'

Janet stepped into the flat and looked around as Les closed the door. 'Where's Tony?' she asked.

'In bed.'

'Is he all right?'

'Yeah. He'll live,' said Les. 'Why don't you go in and say hello?'

'Okay. I will.'

Les knocked on Tony's door then opened it and turned on the light. 'Hey. Steve Stunning. There's somebody here wants to see you.'

Tony half raised his head off the pillows and painfully blinked his eyes open. 'Huh … what?'

'There you go.' Les stood back to let Janet into the room then returned to his seat in the loungeroom, leaving Tony's bedroom door slightly ajar.

'Holy Hannah, Tony. You look a messss.'

Les finished his delicious and was about to make another when Janet came out of Tony's bedroom, switching off the light and closing the door behind her.

'The poor wee fellah,' said Janet. 'How did that happen?'

'Pull up a chair and I'll tell you,' replied Les. 'Would you like a drink?'

'All right. That'd be nice, Les. Bourbon with a beer chaser? Is that okay?'

'Coming right up.'

Janet settled down in the loungeroom and Les made two more bourbons and mineral water. He handed one to Janet plus a bottle of Becks, clinked her glass and sat down opposite her.

'So how did everything start?' asked Janet.

'It was all Ruby's silly bloody boyfriend's fault,' replied Les.

'Richard? Yeah, that'd be right,' said Janet.

Les gave Janet a story about how he walked into the reception with Tony and recognised Richard from the description she gave him. They weren't there very long when Richard saw Tony near the bar, ran up, abused him and started punching into him. With the help of another guest, Les managed to break the fight up then Richard started throwing punches everywhere, hitting a woman. Next thing the reception turned into a giant, humungous brawl. Les could immediately see Tony was in a bad way so he got him out of there as quickly as he could. What happened after that, Les didn't know. They made it to the flats just as the police started to arrive.

'You did the right thing getting Tony out of there,' said Janet.

'Yeah.' Les shook his head. 'Fair dinkum. That Richard's a deadset ratbag.'

'Ohh, tell me about it,' said Janet. 'He's going to finish up in big trouble one day.' She chuckled into her drink. 'He must have bit off more than he could chew during the fight tonight though.'

'Oh, why's that?' Les asked innocently.

'My girlfriend said they took him to hospital with a broken nose and a suspected broken jaw.'

'Good,' said Les. 'Serves him right.'

'My cousin Andrew's in hospital too.'

'Your cousin? I didn't know he was there. What happened to him?'

'He broke his arm,' said Janet. 'He'll be lucky if he doesn't lose his job,' she added. 'He wasn't supposed to be there.'

Les took a sip of bourbon and studied Janet over the glass. 'Putting two and two together, I'd say Andrew told Richard about last night.'

'Oh, for sure,' said Janet. 'They're as thick as thieves those two. In fact I told Ruby something like this might happen.'

'Where is Ruby?'

'Newcastle. Her sister just had twins.'

'Really? Aunty Ruby,' smiled Les. 'It's got a nice ring about it.'

'It has,' Janet smiled back.

Les eased back in his chair. 'So how's your day been, Janet?' he asked. 'And I'm glad you called round tonight. Tony's absolutely no company at all.'

'I can see that,' laughed Janet. 'No. I did lunches at the club. Then I had a jog and went for a swim. I was watching TV and just about to go to bed when my girlfriend rang.'

'How did you get round here? Did you drive?'

'Yeah. But there'll be no cops around tonight. They'll all be down at the reception. Besides, I only live near Elizabeth Beach. Two minutes away.'

'Fair enough.'

Janet held up her empty glass and the empty beer bottle. 'All right if I have another?'

'Sure. Stay there. I'll get them.'

Les got another round of drinks together then sat down and told Janet about his day. He didn't mention her cousin and Richard checking Tony and him out when they were having breakfast. But he told her about his run, the wedding, clicked on his digital camera and showed Janet the photos he'd taken at the Green Cathedral.

'I've been to a few weddings at the Green Cathedral,' said Janet. 'It's beautiful.'

'Yeah. I didn't want to leave,' said Les. 'I can't wait to see the photos Tony took.'

Les and Janet joked and talked about different things and had another round of drinks. Before long they'd moved their chairs closer together and the next thing Les knew, he had his arm around Janet's trim waist and they were kissing each other. After another torrid round of kissing that finished with Norton's hand under Janet's T-shirt, Janet drew back and smiled at Les with her devilish green eyes.

'Have you got any rubbers left, Les?' she asked.

'One,' replied Norton.

'One should be enough.' Janet took another sip of bourbon and placed the glass on the table. 'Les,' she said, 'how would you like to take me into your bedroom, throw me on the bed and get into a bit of good old-fashioned bonking?'

Les studied Janet over his glass for a moment. 'How about I give your snetch a wee suck first?'

'How about you do just that,' smiled Janet.

Les didn't have to throw Janet on the bed. After she took her clothes off, Janet climbed onto the duvet laughing and of her own free will. Les got out of his clothes, placed a towel under one of the rollers to slow down any movement, then spying the little pine cone sticking up, he eased Janet's legs apart and buried his face in it.

After a run and a swim followed by a hot shower, the little pine cone was delightful. Janet squealed and squawked and kicked her legs up and before long she was foaming at the mouth and Mr Wobbly was screaming his nasty little head off demanding in on the action. Les spat out a couple of pubic hairs, slipped Mr Wobbly's little raincoat on, then entered Janet and started pumping away.

With the bed a lot steadier and Les not quite as tired, he was able to give Janet a real good going over. She howled at Les, spurring him on while Les gave it to her from three or four different positions. Finally, Janet got her rocks off with Les going for it dog fashion. So with a great bellow, Les emptied out, leaving Mr Wobbly a quivering, shaking mess once more in his little rubber raincoat.

When they'd finished, Norton went to the bathroom and got rid of the condom before bringing back two glasses of mineral water from the fridge. With the pillows behind them, Les and Janet propped themselves up at the end of the bed, sipped their mineral water and talked about nothing much in particular till Janet eventually looked at her watch.

'Les,' said Janet. 'I'm going to have to love you and leave you. I promised a friend I'd drive her to Laurieton early tomorrow.'

'Okay. I'll walk you down to your car.'

'No. You needn't bother. I'll be all right.'

'Well, at least let me walk you to the door.'

Les had a bit of a perv on Janet putting her clothes back on before he climbed into his T-shirt and jox and walked her to the door. She put her arms round his neck and Les kissed her.

'Don't forget to give me a call when you get back to Sydney, Les,' said Janet.

'No. I will. I'll get the number off Tony.'

'And tell Tony to ring me as well. I want to know how he is. Ruby will be worried too.'

'I'll see that he does.'

Janet kissed Norton then let him go. 'All right, Les,' she said. 'I'll see you when I see you.'

'Goodnight, Janet,' smiled Les. 'Take care of yourself. And thanks for coming round. That was nice of you.'

Janet skipped off down the stairs, Les closed the door and not long after, a car drove off with a slightly noisy muffler. Les yawned and shuffled off to the bathroom.

After drinking a glass of water in the kitchen, Les

turned off his ghetto blaster and all the lights and climbed back into bed. Well, he thought, pushing his head into the pillows. Apart from Steelo getting his head punched in, that wasn't a bad night. I'll definitely give Janet a ring. And if I'm ever up this way again, I'll make sure I see her. She was fun. Les yawned and realised he was tireder than he thought. The scent of Janet's body oil rose from the pillows again and Les had to smile. Yeah. Nothing wrong with Janet, he told himself. She was all right. Seconds later, Norton was out for the count.

Les woke up earlier and feeling better the next morning. He yawned, stretched and had a look out the window; the wind had swung round to the south and it had clouded over with a good chance of rain. Oh well, thought Les. You can't have it perfect all the time. Norton swung his feet out of bed and stepped into the loungeroom. From Tony's room the sound of soft snoring was now a tortured garble as the battered surf photographer sucked air through his mouth and what was left of his nose. Les shook his head sympathetically. I think I might leave sleeping beauty for the time being, he smiled as he went to the bathroom. I just hope that root he had on Tuesday night was a good one.

When he'd finished in the bathroom Les opened the fridge door and peered inside. No, I don't think so, he told himself, closing the door. You can stick the eggplant and a cup of hot water in your arse. I can hear the coffee and eggs calling down the road. Same goes for a run. It's an ideal morning for it. But I just ain't got the time. Les collected his training gear from the back verandah, changed into his blue cargoes and knowing he'd be stuck behind the wheel of his car all day, wore the same maroon T-shirt. He pocketed his money and credit cards, walked down to the Berlina and drove round to Fifty-Fifty.

There weren't many people or cars around this time when Les pulled up outside the restaurant. He got the paper at the supermarket then walked into Fifty-Fifty and ordered what he had for breakfast the day before. The girl behind the counter remembered his craggy smile and in no time Les had a double shot latte sitting in front of him as he opened the paper at the same table he'd shared with Tony. The food arrived and Les enjoyed every mouthful as he read the news. When he paid the bill,

Les ordered two ham and cheese croissants and a large flat white to take away. The girl put everything in a brown paper bag, Les thanked her and drove back to the flat.

Tony was up and in the bathroom when Les walked in the door. He placed the brown paper bag in the kitchen then went to Tony's room and slipped two fifties into Tony's shirt pocket before sitting down in the loungeroom. Eventually Tony stepped out of the bathroom with his grey shorts on and a towel over his shoulder. He was walking stiffly, one eye was completely closed and there was no sign of a smile on his bruised, swollen face.

'G'day, Steelo,' Les said cheerfully. 'How are you feeling this morning, mate?'

Tony looked at Les out of his least blackened eye. 'How am I feeling?' he echoed glumly. 'How do you think I feel? Have a look at my fuckin head.'

'Yes,' agreed Les. 'It wouldn't look out of place in Cirque du Soleil.'

'I think I'd better see a doctor, too. My nose is totally fucked. And I'll probably need some stitches in this cut over my eye. It's still bleeding.'

'Good idea,' replied Les. 'Unfortunately but, old mate, you're going to have to find a doctor without me. I got to piss off. I got a long drive in front of me.'

'That's okay,' said Tony. 'I'll ring Deadline. One of the boys'll give me a lift.'

'There's got to be a doctor down at the shops,' assured Les. 'Or an aromatherapist. You can walk down in five minutes.'

'Yeah,' grunted Tony.

'You hungry?'

'Fuckin starving.'

'Good. I brought you back a couple of croissants and a flat white. They're in the kitchen.'

Tony stepped into the kitchen and opened the brown paper bag. 'Ohh,'thanks, mate,' he said. 'Unreal. What do I owe you?'

Les shook his head. 'Nothing. Do I owe you anything else on the flat? Bond, rent, whatever?'

'No. Everything's sweet.'

'Then we're all square.' Les rose to his feet. 'Okay. I'll leave you to it, Steelo, while I pack my gear.'

Les picked up his ghetto blaster and got his shaving gear from the bathroom; Tony could have what was left of the bourbon and vodka. He then went to his bedroom and packed. Before long Les was back in the loungeroom, his carrybag over his shoulder and his travel bag on the floor. Tony was seated in the kitchen nibbling gingerly on a croissant which he carefully washed down with coffee.

'How are the croissants, Steelo?' asked Les.

'Unreal,' replied Tony. 'I can actually chew the fuckin things. The coffee's good too.'

'Excellent,' smiled Les. 'So when are you going back to Sydney?'

'I got a stack of work on,' replied Tony. 'I should go back tomorrow. But I think I'll stay a couple more days. It's nice up here.'

'Yeah. I don't blame you.'

'I just hope that idiot doesn't come around for a fuckin rematch.'

'Steelo,' winked Les, 'I can guarantee, he won't be around for a rematch.' Les informed Tony what Janet had told him the night before, and also filled in a few in-betweens. When Les had finished, Tony put his coffee down and gave Norton a double blink.

'You mean to tell me,' questioned Tony, 'you put both those cunts in hospital?'

'Steelo,' replied Les from behind a thin smile, 'there's three things in this world you don't do.'

'What's that?'

'You don't piss Superwoman off when she's got her period. You don't park across Bruce Banner's driveway. And you don't put shit on the redheaded terror from Queensland.'

Tony strained and held his ribs. 'Please, Les,' he wheezed. 'Don't make me laugh. I feel shithouse enough as it is.'

Les reached over and shook Tony's hand. 'I'll see you back in Sydney, Steelo.'

'Righto, mate. See you then.'

Les picked up his travel bag and, leaving Tony to finish his breakfast, walked down to the car and threw his bags in the back. He was past the Sailing Club and on his way to Forster when the wind dropped and a light blanket of steady rain fell over everything.

Well, thought Les, as he followed the traffic through the sprawling coastal town, it looks like this is going to settle in. Bugger it. Then again, I suppose they can always do with a bit of rain in the bush. Concentrating on his driving, Les crossed the bridge into Tuncurry then kept going till he passed a sign on the left saying BIG BUZZ AMUSEMENT PARK. A little further on, Les took the overpass and next thing he was on the F3 heading towards Taree and Port Macquarie.

Traffic was slow under the leaden sky. Roadworks were continuous and the rain was little more than an annoying mist before Les would get stuck behind a truck and its massive wheels sprayed muddy water all over the windscreen, blinding him. Great, whinged Les. This looks like being a nice annoying drive all the bloody way. Grinding past another prime mover, Norton mulled over what he knew about Nimbin.

Apart from a grainy old documentary he'd half watched on TV, not a great deal. Some place out in the middle of nowhere, full of tie-dyed hippies with the arse out of their pants, smoking joints and living on lentil burgers. Nothing to get excited about.

Well, if that's the case, pondered Les as he slowed down for another stretch of roadworks, why would anyone want to open a bar there and pay me five hundred dollars a night to play house music? Apart from collecting the dole, hippies haven't got any money. They're not into drinking piss. And the only music they like is Jefferson Airplane, Iron Butterfly and old Joni Mitchell records. Oh well, shrugged Les, clicking the wipers onto intermittent. If this Lonnie's a mate of Eddie's, he must know something. The only thing I have to do is put up with eight hours of doof-doof-fuckin-doof. And take the money and run.

The kilometres and coastal towns ground past in the rain and Les considered putting a tape on. But after listening to all his favourite rock 'n roll tracks then having to put up with two nights of punishing house music, it would kill his spirit. Instead, Les slipped in a talking book Warren's girl had bought for him in an op-shop, partly as a nice thought and partly as a joke: *The Idle Thoughts of an Idle Fellow*, written around the turn of the century by Jerome K. Jerome and now narrated by Peter Joyce. Les slipped in the first of six tapes and adjusted the volume.

All the narrations were introduced by a lumpy oboe and cello, à la *Rumpole of the Bailey*. Then a very English upper-class twit with a priggish Oxford accent would relate his views 'On The Weather', 'On Love', 'On The Blues', 'On Vanity and Vanities'. Etc, etc. Everything seeded with phrases like 'expostulate eloquently', 'a degrading effusiveness', 'ignoble sloth', 'flattery and affectations'. Les found it a load of acerbically amusing bullshit. But it helped pass the time with 'comic dignity' and 'aprobius epitus'.

Les pulled in at Macksville for petrol and bought two diabolical pies, then stopped at Nambucca Heads for a packet of Quick-Eze and a bottle of sparkling mineral water. Coffs Harbour and Grafton went past, along with a few good memories, before Les took a left at Ballina then made it to Lismore and the Nimbin turn-off. Just out of Lismore the rain stopped and he got stuck on a narrow, winding road behind an old grey ute loaded with pipes. It eventually disappeared up a dirt side-road, then in the gloomy mist on the left some spectacular granite cliffs and rocky pinnacles rose out of the lush green valleys. The road climbed through the thick bush and more valleys then Les noticed a sign saying WELCOME TO NIMBIN. REDUCE SPEED. Further on another sign read AN ALCOHOL FREE ZONE EXISTS WITHIN THE VILLAGE OF NIMBIN. It was getting dark when a police station appeared on the left next to a St Vincent de Paul and Les finally reached his destination.

The town was much smaller than Les had expected. He drove past a big garage, a butcher shop, clothing stores and other shops. On the right was the post office, a bakery, a hall and a small arcade. After five hundred metres of old shops with galvanised-iron awnings, the road forked at a war memorial in a small park edged with palm trees. On the right, the local hotel sat on the corner of a narrow lane opposite the Nimbin Hemp Embassy, then the road went down towards where Lonnie told Les he had the bar. Up on the left the road continued past several more shops before disappearing into the surrounding hills. It's too late to check the place out now, thought Les, as he did a U-turn at the war memorial. What I need is a cup of coffee then find a motel. Les parked outside the post office, got his black bomber jacket then locked the car and crossed the road.

The evening was mild and there were people and cars around. But every place Les tried to get a cup of coffee was closing up. Les walked on, passing a white transit van with a blanket over the windscreen, parked back from a low rock wall in front of a big old restaurant with a rainbow on the awning called the Spectrum café. The transit van's side door was open and seated inside, with a huge, plastic bag of dope and a set of scales was an older Aboriginal man with a white beard, wearing khaki shorts and a checked flannelette shirt. It took the man inside the transit van half a second to realise Les was from out of town.

'Hey, bro,' the bearded man called out. 'Want some weed?'

Les looked at the man dumbly for a moment, shook his head then continued on in search of a coffee. Slouched near some bench tables between the rock wall and the Spectrum café was a group of shifty-looking young Aborigines in hooded white tracksuit tops. The tallest of the group noticed Norton's unfamiliar face and stepped out from the others.

'Hey, bro,' said the tall young bloke. 'Want some ganja?'

Les gave him a brief once-up-and-down. 'No thanks,' he replied.

Norton continued on then stopped in front of an estate agency and shook his head. Am I imagining things, he asked himself, or was I just offered dope right out in the open? And was that a police station not far down the road? Christ! If they tried that in Bondi they wouldn't last five minutes. The sniffer dogs'd chew their legs off.

Near the estate agency was a newsagent and a large restaurant and pizza parlour. Les stepped inside for a coffee and got told the machine wasn't on. Come back in half-an-hour. Les walked outside and went into the estate agency. Seated behind a desk was a grey-haired man wearing a white shirt and blue trousers.

'Excuse me, boss,' asked Les. 'But where's the nearest motel.'

'Lismore,' replied the man.

'Lismore?' said Les.

'Yeah. We don't have a motel in Nimbin. There's a backpackers lodge further down the road. Or the hotel caters for backpackers. You'd be better off in the hotel. It's closer to town.'

'Backpackers?' said Les.

'That's right.'

'Thanks, mate.'

Les stepped out onto the footpath and stared over at the pub. It was a big wooden colonial-style hotel, painted blue, with a wide verandah that overlooked the street. The entrance was on the corner opposite the Hemp Embassy, and at the other end of the hotel a set of steps ran up alongside a steep, narrow driveway separating the hotel from a couple of clothing shops set behind trees. Les took a deep breath and crossed the road.

Grouped around the entrance were three shifty-looking Aborigines, older than the ones near the rock wall, wearing dark tracksuits. As Les approached, one of the group stepped up to Les. He had a surly face under a crop of untidy brown hair and was wearing a dark blue tracksuit with distinctive red piping along the sleeves.

'Hey, bro,' he said bluntly. 'Want some weed?'

Les gave him a tight shake of his head. 'No.'

The man looked at Norton as if he'd just insulted him by declining his offer, then rejoined his mates. Fair dinkum, thought Les, stepping into the hotel. The next cunt that offers me a bag of dope I'm going to kick him fair in the nuts.

The hotel was big inside with a well-stocked bar featuring a number of beers on tap. A wide-screen TV and a bank of TAB screens sat above the entrance and there was no shortage of stools and tables. The bar angled round on the right to an empty dining room that led to an open loungeroom at the back of the hotel. Facing the bar, a curved doorway led to another loungeroom with a pool table on one side and a bank of poker machines on the other. In between was a dancefloor, a mirror ball and a low stage with a DJ booth. Hanging from one wall a sign read TONIGHT — TEN PIECE DRUM BAND. On the wall behind the dancefloor was a large red banner with SAMBA SARDANA blazed across the front in white with yellow edging. Half-a-dozen solid men were seated drinking at the public bar and serving them was a dark-haired girl wearing a black T-shirt. Alongside her was a beefy man with dark hair and a salt and pepper beard wearing a blue Toohey's polo shirt. Les walked up to the man with the beard.

'Yeah. What can I get you?' smiled the man.

'Can I have a room for three nights?' asked Les.

The man gave Les a bit of a once-up-and-down. 'Sure,' he replied. 'Twenty-five bucks a night. Can you pay cash? The computer's shit itself.'

'Yeah. No problems,' shrugged Les, pulling seventy-five dollars out of his shorts.

The bloke in the polo shirt got a ledger from an office at the end of the bar, wrote Les out a receipt and handed him two keys tied to a tab. He explained one key was to his room. The other let him into the hotel. One entrance was at the top of the stairs alongside the laneway. The other was on the verandah behind the hotel and there was a parking area down the laneway. Things were quiet at the moment, so he should have the room to himself.

Les nodded to the dining room. 'When can I get a meal?' he asked.

'You can't,' replied the bloke. 'The cook broke his leg in a car accident. And the waitress pissed off to the Gold Coast with one of the cleaners.'

'Fair enough,' said Les.

'The pizza joint across the road's got a restaurant. The food's all right. Stick your head in there.'

'Okay,' said Les, picking up the keys.

'Enjoy your stay in Nimbin,' smiled the bloke, placing Norton's money in the ledger.

'I'm sure I will,' replied Les.

Norton left the hotel and walked up to his car. He did a U-turn then drove back and hung a right down the laneway, coming out in a small, grassy car park heavy with evening dew. Les pulled up next to a couple of mud-spattered utilities then got out and had a look around in the soft light from the hotel.

A set of stairs led up to the cellar, another to the loungeroom behind the dining room and another set ran up to a verandah with a door on the right. Les got his bags, locked the car and climbed the stairs till he reached the verandah. The key fitted easily and Les stepped into a gloomy corridor with blue carpet and green walls.

On the left was the Gents toilets and showers. Opposite was the Ladies. The corridor led to another with rooms running left and right. Les slid the key into room 19 on the right, found the light switch then stepped inside and closed the door behind him.

Twenty-five dollars a night got Norton a small clean room with green walls and two tubular steel double bunks on either side. There was a narrow bench as you walked in with a kitchen tidy beneath it, and between where the bunks sat against the far wall was another door. Les tossed his bags on the top right bunk, then slipped the bolt on the second door and stepped outside onto a long wide verandah with a scattering of chairs and tables sitting on a solid wooden floor with solid wooden railings.

The verandah gave an uninterrupted view of Nimbin's main street and Les was peering towards the Lismore end of town when two banks of arc lights near the door came on, lighting up the immediate area in front of the hotel. Les stared out into the brightness for a moment then walked back into his room, bolting the door behind him.

What did Lonnie say? Les asked himself, as he sat down on the bottom left bunk and stared across at the other one. Book into the pub. He's got to be fuckin kidding. This is all right if your name's Olaf and you wear socks and sandals and a bandana tied round your head and you're on a budget. But I'm not a fuckin backpacker. I own a house. I got money in the bank. And I can afford a modicum of luxury. Les wistfully shook his head. Oh well, he smiled thinly. Look on the bright side. The bloke behind the bar said things are quiet so I should have the room to myself. On the weekend you can bet I'll be sharing it with two Japs who stink of miso soup and a Pommy who hasn't had a bath since the Kelly gang rode out of Jerilderie. Boy! Can I find them. Anyway. Fuck it. I'm here now. Let's go and have a bite to eat. Les locked his room and followed the corridor left to a set of carpeted stairs that angled down to the side entrance. He took the stairs to the door, opened it and followed a set of wooden stairs down to the street.

The pizza shop was fairly big. A counter faced the door when you walked in and an arched doorway on the left led to a dining room. Two people were seated next to a drink machine, waiting for pizzas. Les picked up a menu from the counter and ordered a smoked salmon salad, spaghetti bolognaise and a flat white from a young girl in black. After paying up front, he found a table in the dining room, plonked himself down on a wooden loop-backed chair and had a cursory look around.

Pinned to the walls were a number of gaudy little paintings, windows faced the street and a door on the right led to a narrow alleyway. Alongside him a beefy European family of four was scoffing four monstrous pizzas and three family-size bottles of Coke. Seated in front of the windows, another family was checking out a bag of dope. One of the family rolled a joint then he and another man slipped out the side door. Norton's coffee arrived and while he sipped it, he debated whether to ring Lonreghan. If he did, Lonnie would probably want him to come down to the bar where he'd no doubt find him something to do. And if Les did go down, he'd probably tell Lonnie what he thought of his accommodation arrangements. No, fuck him, thought Les. I'll ring him tomorrow. Les looked up as the waitress arrived with both the smoked salmon and the spaghetti.

The food was good and there was plenty of it. Les got through the smoked salmon, but no matter how hard he tried, he couldn't finish the spaghetti bolognaise. Shit! That's got to be a first, smiled Les, placing his knife and fork on the plate and pushing it away. He sat at the table for a moment and found himself yawning and rubbing his eyes; the long drive in the rain had left him drained. The best thing to do now, figured Les, is have a few drinks and try to knock myself out so I can sleep in that bunk. He got up, left a tip, then walked the short distance back to the hotel.

There were about a dozen at the bar and a bit of a crowd in the loungeroom waiting for the band to start. Two couples were shuffling around on the dancefloor to some low-key house music. Les hung at the loungeroom door for a moment to check out the punters. He couldn't see any tie-dyed hippies wearing crushed velvet or love beads. More an older crowd in jeans, T-shirts, tracksuits, coloured or plain dresses and jackets. Some women wore high-heeled boots, most of the punters wore trainers and here and there the odd funny hat. Les ordered a middy of Carlton and a Jack Daniel's and soda, then sat down under the TV and absently watched a game of rugby union on Sky channel. Les was on his third beer and another Jack Daniel's and starting to mellow out when the music stopped in the loungeroom and seconds later it sounded like the end of the world. He got up from his table and took his drinks across to the lounge.

Up on stage were ten fired-up men and women in bright red outfits banging away on huge red drums and other percussion instruments. One girl wore a red tutu, two had black afros, the rest wore gaudy red hats or boas and out front, banging furiously on a silver drum, was a fiendish-looking man in a black top hat with a red ostrich feather pinned to the front. And they were putting everything into it, making enough noise to bring the roof down and raise the dead at the same time. With a big smile on his face, Les watched from the doorway then found a spot near the dancefloor and started bopping away to himself, stopping now and again to go to the bar.

Samba Sardana ended their first bracket to much cheering and whistling from the appreciative crowd. Les finished his drinks, got a fresh round, then went back to where he'd been sitting beneath the TV.

He was half on the nod and only drinking bourbon when the band returned.

Samba Sardana's second bracket was even louder than the first. The leader in the top hat would blow a whistle, they'd all stop, he'd blow it again and with perfect timing they'd all come in on cue and start banging away, chock full of enthusiasm. It was hard to tell who was enjoying themselves the most — the drummers or the punters. The band finally banged out their last number, thanked the crowd and filed off stage right to more whistling and cheering. Les finished his last bourbon and decided it was well and truly time to file off stage right himself. He walked through the dining room, wearily climbed the stairs by the open-air lounge, then let himself in the back door. The band was getting changed in two rooms down the corridor from Les and as he went past, Les gave them a boozy smile and told them how much he enjoyed their performance. They thanked him for the compliment and Norton went to his room.

Yawning non-stop, Les changed into his old blue tracksuit and decided to sleep on the bottom bunk opposite the one he tossed his bag on. After a quick test, Les was pleased to find the mattress was comfortable and the pillows and duvet were clean and fresh. Oh well, smiled Les, staring up at the top bunk, even though it feels like I'm sleeping in a submarine, things could be a lot worse. He got up and switched off the light. Les needn't have bothered. The arc lights on the verandah reflected through the glass panes on the adjacent door, lighting his room up like the middle of the day. Did I just say something? scowled Les. He got a black T-shirt from his travel bag, doubled it over, then lay down and placed it over his eyes. It helped considerably, and sleeping in a submarine or not, it wasn't long before Norton was snoring his head off.

Les didn't quite know what was going on when he woke up the next morning. 'What the …?' He removed the T-shirt and blinked up at the bunk above him as everything fell into place. 'Oh shit!' he said, running a dry tongue over his lips. After a moment or two, he swung his legs over the bunk, yawned, then stood up and stretched, pleased to find his hangover wasn't as bad as he thought it would be. 'Bloody hell! Look at the time.' Les got his towel, shaving kit, two Panadeine and a clean pair of jox and headed for the bathroom.

There was no one around and the bathroom was clean with plenty of hot water. Les didn't bother about a shave, but had a good long shower then went back to his room and changed into his black cargoes and a white 99.9 FM T-shirt he bought in Victor Harbor. Now, what's the day doing? he asked himself, once he'd laced on his trainers. Les unbolted the door and stepped out onto the verandah.

Plenty of fat white clouds were drifting around in the breeze. But the sun was shining brightly and there was no sign of rain. Cars were coming and going and people were walking around and Nimbin appeared to have come to life as the morning headed towards noon. Les strolled down to the far end of the verandah and noticed you didn't have to drive far before the town ended in a rolling maze of mountains and valleys. Walking back, he stared over at a building near the pizza shop. Written a little unevenly above the awning was THINK GLOBALLY ACT LOCALLY TO SAVE THE ENDANGERED SPECIES NIMBIN INDEPENDENT POWER ACTION A COMMUNITY PARTNERSHIP EXHIBITING SOLUTIONS TO CLIMATE CHANGE. Fair enough, smiled Les. We all must do our bit to save the planet. Les walked down to the other end of the verandah and gazed across the laneway at the Nimbin Hemp Embassy. The awning was painted bright red and printed below the Nimbin Hemp Embassy sign was WE ARE NOT CRIMINALS.

From the hotel verandah, Les had an excellent and inconspicuous view of the street below where he could hear everything that was going on. The pungent odour of someone smoking pot drifted up through the floorboards and made Les poke his head over the railing. The Aborigine in the dark blue tracksuit who had offered Les dope the evening before was standing outside the hotel with his mates drinking cans of UDL and one of the group was smoking a joint. A pimply-faced white kid in a pair of baggy check shorts and a black T-shirt came across the road with an expectant look on his face. One of the group wearing a grey tracksuit top picked up on the kid's expression and immediately approached him.

'Want some weed, bro?' he asked.

'Yeah,' the kid replied vaguely.

'Well, just come down here away from the cameras.'

Les watched them disappear down the laneway and stepped back from the railing. Well there you go, he smiled. Nice to see a group of indigenous small businessmen making a well-earned dollar. I wonder if the cans of UDL and the hot one attract a fringe benefits tax? His stomach rumbling with hunger, Les went back to his room. The Spectrum Café across the road looked as good as anywhere. Les got his money and credit cards and walked down to the front entrance. After stopping for the morning paper, he strolled along to the café. The folding wooden door at the front was wide open so Les stepped straight through.

Inside, the old eatery was big and gloomy with a blackboard menu behind a long counter on the right that faced a row of bench tables and chairs set against the opposite wall. Beneath the counter was a glass cabinet stacked with cakes, and a refrigerated drink container stood beneath the blackboard. At the back of the restaurant an open door led to a grassy area edged with trees. Several chairs and tables sat in the middle and seated around them, rolling or smoking joints, were a few sour-faced old hippies with beards and long straggly hair, dressed like relics left over from the age of Aquarius. One in particular, with drooping eyes and a long grey beard, reminded Les of Rip Van Winkle — the man in the fairy tale who fell asleep for a hundred years.

Les left the relics to it and stepped across to the counter. After a quick look at the blackboard menu, he ordered scrambled eggs and bacon, plus a flat white, from a beefy, pleasant-faced man in black with his hair pulled back in a ponytail, who assured him it wouldn't take long. There was only one other person in the café, a skinny brunette in a long red dress drinking coffee. Les chose a table one back from the doorway so he could read his paper and check out the punters walking past at the same time. He spread his paper out as the cutlery and paper napkins arrived, then thought of something. Les left his paper on the table and walked back to the counter for a bottle of sparkling mineral water. When he got back to his table his paper had gone.

'What the fuck!'

Les scowled around the café. The woman drinking coffee didn't have it and there was no one else around except the hippies out the back. And even if one of them did take his paper, it would be pointless going out and putting the heavies on them in their condition. All Norton could do was storm up to the newsagent and get another one. Jesus! They're not bad around here, gritted Les as he left the café. He returned with another paper just as his coffee arrived.

The coffee was quite good. The food arrived promptly and it wasn't too bad either with plenty of crisp buttered toast and tiny packets of jam. Les was chomping away, half reading the paper and half watching the people walking past, when a man seated on one of the bench tables in front of the café, reading a magazine and wearing jeans and a white T-shirt with NIMBIN UNIVERSITY on the front caught his eye. He had thinning dark hair going grey, a full face with a pronounced dimple in his chin, and Les found himself trying to think of someone in Bondi the man reminded him of. Les was mulling this over as he chewed on a slice of toast when a woman came past on the right wearing a white chef's jacket and carrying a plastic bag full of carrots.

'Morning, Gazza,' she said.

The man glanced up from his magazine. 'Hey, Nina,' he smiled. 'How's things?'

'Ohh, can't complain.'

'Good on you.'

The woman continued on her way and the man called Gazza returned to his magazine while Les absently studied him over his coffee. Next thing an Aboriginal man appeared on the left wearing a pair of cream trousers and a yellow check shirt. He had scrubby brown hair and didn't look much like an

Aborigine. But Les figured him to be a blackfellah because he was carrying two placards. One read: SORRY IS A HOLLOW WORD. A BILL OF RIGHTS MAKES IT SOLID. The other read: WE ARE NOT FAUNA. GIVE US A BILL OF RIGHTS. The man with the signs stopped at Gazza's table.

'G'day, Gazza,' he said directly.

Gazza glanced up impassively from his magazine. 'Morning, Jimmy,' he replied. Then he noticed the two placards. 'Hello. What the fuck's all this about?'

'I'm protesting.'

'You're protesting? Christ! What about this time?' Gazza read the two placards out loud then shook his head. 'Fuckin hell! You're not fair dinkum, are you?'

'Why wouldn't I be?' replied Jimmy, placing the placards on the table.

Either Gazza was in a bad mood or Jimmy had touched a nerve. But Gazza threw his magazine on the table and stared in open disbelief. 'Jesus Christ, Jimmy,' he said. 'You've been whingeing about Sorry for I don't know how many fuckin years. Now you got it. And it's still not good enough.'

Jimmy ignored Gazza. 'I want a treaty. And I want social justice,' he said.

'A treaty and social justice,' echoed Gazza. 'Fair dinkum, Jimmy. What don't you fuckin want? You want social justice. Reconciliation. Assimilation. Dialogue. Land rights. Mineral rights. Native Title. Native council. An indigenous bill of rights. A United Nations Declaration of Rights. Mabo. Wik. Land councils. Then there's the Stolen Generation. Black deaths in custody. Customary law. Indigenous law. Racial discrimination.' Gazza nodded to the placards. 'Now this. Fuck me, mate. Does it ever end?'

'And I want compensation for past grievances,' continued Jimmy.

'Compensation for past grievances. Yeah,' nodded Gazza. 'In other words, money. Well, if you wanted money, why didn't you get some of the billions of dollars your mates in ATSIC pissed up against the wall in a flood of nepotism?' Gazza looked directly at Jimmy. 'You do know what nepotism is, don't you, Jimmy?'

'Of course I know what nepotism is,' replied Jimmy. 'I'm a blackfellah. I've had to suffer it all my life.'

'No. That's racism, you fuckin goose,' said Gazza. 'It means looking after your mates.'

'Because of whitefellah law, all me mates are in gaol.'

'Well, if they didn't sell dope and rob and bash people, they probably wouldn't be in gaol. You fuckin moron.'

Les watched in astonishment as Gazza abused and berated the inoffensive Aboriginal man for doing no more than make a legitimate protest. In the meantime a small crowd had started to gather in front of the café.

'You stole me country,' said Jimmy.

'Stole your country?' howled Gazza. 'Ohh, get fucked, Jimmy. If your silly fuckin Abo mates back in 1788 had brains enough to invent a bow and arrow, the First Fleet wouldn't have landed. All they had to take on was a bunch of half-starved Royal Marines armed with old muskets. A couple of dozen Apache Indians would have sorted them out in ten minutes. And you're lucky it was the Poms and not the Spanish who sailed in through the Heads, you ungrateful prick of a thing. They'd have given you native fuckin title. Just like they gave the Indians in South America. You'd've all been worked to death by now.'

'I also want,' continued Jimmy, 'open admission of disenfranchisement and white guilt. And constitutional recognition of my Aboriginal identity.'

'Aboriginal identity.' Gazza threw his hands in the air. 'Fair dinkum! Have you had a look in the mirror lately, Jimmy? You've got about as much blackfellah in you as Miss Iceland. You cunt.'

Jimmy ignored Gazza. 'And I ain't finished there,' he stated. 'I'm also demanding …'

Les turned to his left as the man with the ponytail appeared from behind the counter and pushed the shutter door across. 'I'll close the door a bit,' he said. 'Things are getting a little heated out there.'

'Fair enough,' smiled Les.

'Good thing they're both sober.'

With the front door almost closed, the café was virtually left in darkness. Les quietly finished his coffee in the dim glow of a few small sunken lights in the ceiling then, taking his paper with him this time, walked across to the counter and ordered another flat white. Returning to his table, Les found his last piece of toast and packet of strawberry jam was gone. The woman in the long dress had left and the hippies were all down the back getting stoned.

'Strike me hooray,' said Les, looking under his table. 'What have they fuckin got in here? Elves?'

The man brought Norton's coffee over then tentatively opened the front door. Jimmy and Gazza were gone and the small crowd had dispersed. 'Thank God for that,' the man said.

Les finished his coffee and paper, paid the bill and stepped out onto the footpath. Well, he thought, glancing at his watch, I might take a quick look around, then ring my mate Lonnie. He's probably wondering where I am. Les dumped his paper in a bin, turned left and followed the shops to where they finished at a corner past the war memorial, then worked his way back.

Apart from an old supermarket, the newsagency and a few others, it was mostly small souvenir shops selling T-shirts and whatever all with a marijuana theme and everything on the T-shirts from BEWARE THE NIMBIN BISCUIT to THE NIMBIN HEMP OLYMPICS. Alongside the Spectrum Café was the Nimbin Museum. Les dropped a donation in an old milk can and stepped inside an old dusty wooden building.

Cut away kombi wagons full of junk were stacked against the walls along with newspaper photos and articles about hippies smoking pot or getting busted for doing it. A sign in one room read NO DEALING OR SMOKING DRUGS IN THE MUSEUM. In the next room a fat, good-natured Aboriginal woman and two younger ones had a bong going, and Les got three offers to buy dope. Norton left the museum then stopped in front of another souvenir shop to read what was written across the front window:

BUSINESS HOURS: OPEN MOST DAYS ABOUT 11–12,
OCCASIONALLY AS EARLY AS 9 BUT SOME DAYS AS
LATE AS 2 OR 3. WE CLOSE AT 5.30 OR 6 —
OCCASIONALLY AT 4 OR 5 BUT SOMETIMES AS LATE
AS 10 OR 11 — SOME DAYS WE ARE NOT HERE AT
ALL. BUT … LATELY I'VE BEEN HERE JUST ABOUT
ALL THE TIME … EXCEPT WHEN I'M SOMEPLACE
ELSE BUT I SHOULD BE HERE THEN TOO …

Very good, opined Les. Obviously penned by a free spirit, not confined by the shackles of corporate orthodoxy.

Les drifted around till he finished up in the Nimbin Hemp Embassy. It was another big old wooden building with a glass counter in the middle, surrounded by marijuana paraphernalia, hemp clothing and T-shirts. In one corner a video showed some bearded man seated at a table, tossing around several kilograms of heads like big green corn cobs. A door on the right led to another room where several backpackers were seated along a wooden counter avidly mulling up.

Norton's attitude to dope was fairly ambiguous. Of all the drugs going around, pot, grown out in the open, was the most innocuous. And arresting citizens in their own homes for just having a smoke and listening to music, while junkies were robbing houses and bashing old ladies, and kids were frying their brains on methamphetamine and ice, didn't make much sense. Also, hemp, the non-smoking type, was a plant that had been around for thousands of years and could easily stop the destruction of rainforests for paper, while producing oil, clothing and myriad other products at the same time. But seeing marijuana paraphernalia everywhere and having it shoved in your face by shifty-looking dope dealers, got to be a turn-off. Nevertheless, Norton bought three souvenir T-shirts. A black one for Warren, with 007 JAMES BONG LICENSED TO CHILL on the front. A brown one with NIMBIN UNIVERSITY on it for Warren's girlfriend Beatrice. And a grey one for himself with RAINBOW LANE: MY FAVOURITE ADDRESS IN NIMBIN on the front.

With his T-shirts in a brown paper bag, Les stepped out of the Hemp Embassy to cross over to the hotel and fell in alongside a barrel-chested old bloke in a pair of white shorts and a baggy green T-shirt videoing the shops and the hotel. He had a mop of snow-white hair and a pair of steel-rimmed glasses perched beneath a domed forehead. Next to him was his grey-haired wife, wearing a white tracksuit and huge wraparound sunglasses that covered her spectacles. They looked European and

Les overheard them talking to each other in English with a foreign accent.

The old bloke was happily videoing away when he strolled past the Aborigine in the blue tracksuit who had offered Les dope, who was standing at the edge of the footpath outside the hotel with his two mates. Blue tracksuit was obviously the leader of the gang and as soon as he spotted the old bloke with the video camera, his face reddened.

'Hey,' he shouted angrily. 'Is that fuckin thing on?'

The old bloke stopped, turned to his wife then turned back to Blue Tracksuit. 'I am sorry,' he said quietly. 'I do not understand.'

'I said, is that fuckin thing on?' Blue Tracksuit shouted again.

The old woman nervously took hold of her husband's arm while they stood facing Blue Tracksuit and his mates. 'What is wrong?' she asked her husband.

'I don't want my privacy filmed all round the fuckin world,' yelled Blue Tracksuit. 'Fuck off. You nosy old cunt.'

His video camera still absently rolling, the old bloke turned to his wife. 'Is all right,' he assured her. 'Do not be frightened.'

'I'll tell you what,' snarled Blue Tracksuit, 'you want something to video? Go and get your granddaughter and you can film me fucking her. How about that?'

The wife paled while the old man's body stiffened. His face turrned to stone and a glint of pure loathing suddenly burned in his eyes towards the man in the blue tracksuit. Les strolled past the old bloke and his wife, before stopping at the bottom of the stairs.

'Ahh, don't take any notice of the old cunt, Ray,' said one of Blue Tracksuit's mates. 'He's only a mug.'

'Fuck him,' spat Blue Tracksuit. 'Who's he think he fuckin is?'

The old bloke continued to stare at Blue Tracksuit before stepping off the footpath and guiding his wife across the road.

'Ohh, what are you looking at, you fuckin old goose?' said Blue Tracksuit. 'Go on. Fuck off.'

The old bloke took his wife across to a white Winnebago with a red, white and blue flag in the corner of the rear window, parked alongside the war memorial. After opening the far door to let his wife in, the old bloke came round to the driver's side. He stared at Blue Tracksuit for a moment as one of the hood's mates left to do a deal, then got behind the wheel and drove off. Les watched the van disappear before climbing the stairs and opening the side door.

Fair enough, mused Les, when he reached the corridor. You can't go videoing the lovable local indigenous persons like that. You might steal their spirituality. Of course videoing that foul-mouthed prick and his mates dealing dope in the main street wouldn't help their spirits much either. Les shook his head as he stepped inside his room. So much for peace, love and lentil burgers. From what I've seen so far, this place is fucked. Les tossed his souvenir T-shirts on the top bunk and put the distasteful incident outside the hotel behind him. He took out his mobile phone, clicked it on then found Lonnie Lonreghan's number and dialled.

'Hello. Lonnie speaking.'

'G'day, Lonnie. It's Les Norton.'

'Les. Hey. How are you, mate?'

'Not bad.'

'Shit. I'm glad you called,' said Lonnie. 'I was starting to get a bit worried.'

'Yeah. Well I've been settling in,' replied Les. 'Finding my way around the city.'

'How's the hotel?'

'Oh, it's good,' said Les, kicking one of the bunks.

'Room service is a bit slow. But the entertainment's been unreal.'

Lonnie chuckled quietly into the phone. 'So where are you now? At the hotel?'

'Yes. Relaxing in my suite.'

'Well, I'm at the bar. Why don't you come down and we'll go over a few things about tonight? You know where it is?'

'Yeah. Give me about fifteen minutes.'

'Righto, Les. See you then.'

Les hung up and looked at his mobile. Was there anyone else he wanted to ring? Not particularly. He switched it off and placed it in his overnight bag. After tidying one or two things up in his room, Norton left the hotel and headed for the bar.

The Double L Ranch was a quick downhill walk past the clothes shops next to the laneway, set back a few metres from the road between two vacant allotments across from a community centre surrounded by trees. Maybe it was the effect Lonnie wanted. Les wasn't quite sure. But the bar was no more than a big, rough slab hut with a galvanised-iron roof. There was a solid double door on the right, and on the left was a small parking area and delivery bay, where a silver Holden Colorado sat alongside an old black VW. Two wooden poles joined at the top by a length of weathered timber with DOUBLE L RANCH burnt into it, stood above a short concrete path leading to the front door. A couple of windows with security grilles looked out over the parking area. There was no landscaping or any sign of colour. Les gave the drab venue a quick perusal then followed the path to the entrance, pushed open the door on the left and stepped inside.

Les found himself in a narrow foyer with a small counter facing the double doors and an archway on the left. Les walked through the archway to find the inside of the club matched the outside. There was no ceiling, just beams and trusses holding up the lighting and the galvanised-iron roof with room underneath for a hundred people maximum. On the right was a bar with a mirror running along the wall behind and the door to an office at the foyer end. The bar finished where the room angled round to a kitchen that stood alongside a fire escape door and also faced the toilets in the opposite corner. Plain blue carpet covered the floor, beneath a smattering of wooden tables and stools, and several bench tables and seats sat beneath the windows facing the street. Poked in a corner on the left was a disc jockey's booth and Les counted six Bose speakers amongst the lights hanging from the beams. He couldn't see a mirror ball and there didn't appear to be a dancefloor. Les turned to his right.

Standing in front of the bar, a man wearing jeans and a blue polo shirt with the Double L logo on the pocket was talking quietly to three women. The man was about average height and build, with untidy black hair pushed across a creased face, and he had a wall eye. Les stared at the man and a striking comparison kicked straight in. Detective Columbo. The only things missing were the half-smoked cigar and the crumpled grey coat. Standing on the man's right was a plump blonde also wearing jeans and a blue polo shirt, and on his left was a spiky-haired brunette dressed the same. Behind the bar stood a well-stacked blonde in a black dress holding an A4 lecture pad. The group suddenly noticed Les and stopped whatever it was they were doing. Les walked straight over to the man with the wall eye.

'Are you Lonnie Lonreghan?' asked Les.

'Yeah, yeah,' smiled the man, tapping absently at his forehead. 'You got to be Les.'

'That's right,' replied Les, offering his hand. 'Nice to meet you, Lonnie.'

'Good to meet you too, Les.' The man shook Norton's hand then turned to the three women.

'Ladies,' he said. 'This is Les Norton. Our swingin DJ for the next two nights. Les, this is Kerrie, my bar manager.' Les shook hands and exchanged pleasantries with the blonde behind the bar. 'And this is Robyn and Tania, my ace bar staff.' Les shook hands with Robyn, the plump blonde, and Tania, the brunette. 'I also got a bar useful called Jock. And two guys on the door, Mason and Buddy. You'll meet them tonight. They're good lads.'

'Fair enough,' nodded Les.

Lonnie pointed to the lecture pad the bar manager was holding. 'Kerrie, will you check those figures again, while I show Les around.'

'Sure, Lonnie,' she replied.

'You want a drink, Les?' asked Lonnie.

'I wouldn't mind a sparkling mineral water,' replied Les.

'Kerrie.'

Kerrie nodded then reached down and got Les a small bottle of mineral water from a cabinet. Les thanked her, then, sipping from the bottle, followed Lonnie around while he pointed various things out. There wasn't much to see and Les found what there wasn't to be quite an eye-opener.

Behind the rough wooden bar, spirits were very basic, there were no beers on tap and the glass cabinets contained one brand of alco-pops, three brands of Australian beer and one German. Soft drinks consisted of Coca-Cola, lemonade and mineral water. The office was as big as Norton's laundry at home and contained a safe pushed against the wall beneath a small table, a white board, a battery powered clock, a computer, and an office chair.

Stepping out from behind the bar, Les found the Double L kitchen wasn't much bigger than the office, and sold pies and hamburgers which could be washed down with instant coffee or tea bags. Above the pie warmer a small sign read CHIPS AND GRAVY. TOAST AND GRAVY. GRAVY. A small till sat on the counter and a sliding door on the back wall led to the fridge and storeroom.

The urinal in the Gents was two halves of a forty-four gallon drum on a concrete stand with a garden hose below and a cistern above. There was one metal toilet bowl and a metal sink with a hand dryer and no mirror. The lighting was dim, the concrete floor was badly laid and poorly drained and the only difference between the Double L's Gents and something from a third world country was that the Double L's hadn't seen any action yet.

Lonnie gave Les a quick tour of the stools and tables then led him over to the DJ booth, which stood a metre above the floor and was built from more old wood. Three steps led up to a half-door where you gained entrance and Les was about to follow Lonnie up the steps when he noticed a small sign across the front of the DJ booth in white letters with red edging. THIS IS NOT A RAVE. THERE IS NO DANCEFLOOR. DANCING STRICTLY PROHIBITED. OFFENDERS WILL BE EJECTED. BY ORDER. THE MANAGEMENT. Les read the sign again before stepping into the DJ booth behind Lonnie.

It was cramped and spartan. But the components were brand new and top of the range. Two CD players sat between a powerful amplifier and a computer, while stacked neatly on shelves below were hundreds of CDs in easily accessible racks. There was a small lamp, no microphone, no headphones and set into the console on the right-hand side of the computer was a solid yellow switch.

'Basically, Les,' said Lonnie, waving his hand over everything, 'all I want you to do is record every track you play.'

'Record all the tracks,' said Les.

'Yeah. They'll go onto the computer. Later I'll transfer them to an MP 3. Then burn them onto a CD.' Lonnie picked out a CD. The Rolling Stones' *A Bigger Bang*. 'You see on the back, I've put a dot next to different tracks with a white marking pen?'

'Yeah,' nodded Les.

'Well, they're the tracks I want you to record.'

'Any particular order?'

'Nope. Just play them at random. And you don't have to write them down. The computer will read and record everything.'

'Cool,' said Les.

Lonnie slipped the CD into the player and seconds later 'Rough Justice' came thumping out of the Bose speakers, filling every corner of the room, clear as a bell.

'Holy smoke!' acknowledged Les. 'That's a bloody good sound system.'

'Yeah. It's not bad,' agreed Lonnie. 'The place isn't all that big. So just keep the amp at half volume.'

'Righto.'

Lonnie ran Les over the controls a couple of times and Les soon figured out you didn't have to be a rocket scientist to do what Lonnie asked. It was no harder than making tapes on his stereo at home. Lonnie pressed the stop button, took the CD out and placed it back with the others.

'Any questions?' asked Lonnie.

'Yeah,' nodded Les. 'What's the yellow switch for?'

Lonnie flicked the yellow switch up and a red sign flashed on and off between the windows facing the car park: DANCING PROHIBITED. STOP.

'If any cunt starts dancing,' said Lonnie, 'push the yellow switch. And if they don't stop, I'll get the boys to throw them out. And if anyone says anything to you, tell them there's no dancefloor. And if they don't like it, they can fuck off. But I'll be keeping an eye on things from behind the bar.'

'Are they allowed to tap their feet or clap their hands?' Les asked.

'A little bit,' nodded Lonnie

Les looked at Lonnie in disbelief. 'Lonnie,' he said. 'For the life of me I can't figure this out. You're running a nightclub with a top sound system and by eleven o'clock it's going to be full of drunks and mullheads. Yet you won't let anyone boogie. What …?'

'I know. It's a funny one,' said Lonnie. 'But I'll explain everything to you when Eddie gets here on Saturday night.'

Les shook his head. 'All right.'

Lonnie put an arm around Norton's shoulder and in a fatherly fashion led him out of the DJ cabinet to one of the tables out the front. 'Well. What do you reckon about the place, Les?' he asked, waving an arm around the bar.

'What do I reckon?' said Les, placing his empty bottle on the table.

'Yeah. What do you think of the joint?'

Seeing he was only going to be there two nights Les thought he might as well tell Lonnie the truth. 'It's a fuckin dump,' replied Les. 'You got fuck all to drink. Fuck all to eat. You've built the joint out of old railway sleepers and whatever else you could scrounge up. There's no dancing. No vibe. And I hope to Christ my bladder can hold out for four hours, because once that brasco gets a roll on, you'll catch anything in there from bubonic plague to the jack.' Les looked directly at Lonnie. 'The joint's a dump.'

Les expected Lonnie to tell him to get well and truly fucked and don't bother turning up later. Instead his face broke into a happy grin.

'I know,' agreed Lonnie. 'Isn't it a shit fight? If I didn't own the joint, I wouldn't be seen dead in here.'

'Well, what the fuck's going on?'

'Like I said, Les,' smiled Lonnie, 'I'll explain everything to you when Eddie gets here on Saturday night.'

'Including why I'm staying in a backpacker's hotel. Because fair dinkum, Lonnie, I don't need the money. I'm only here returning Eddie a favour.'

'I know that, Les. And I truly appreciate it.'

'So where do you live?' Les asked.

Lonnie nodded towards the road. 'On an old farm. About thirty-five clicks out of town.'

'Okay.' Les paused for a second. 'All right, Lonnie,' he said. 'I'll see you tonight. Eight o'clock.'

Lonnie gave Les a warm handshake. 'I'll see you then, mate. And thanks again.'

'No worries.' Les waved the girls goodbye and left the room.

Outside, Les stood quietly in the sun for a moment, then looked back at the venue. That place is a madhouse, he told himself. And the owner needs his head read. The punters'll tar and feather me tonight if I have to hit that yellow No Dancing switch. Boy! Can I get myself into some shit.

Les turned to his right and noticed the road levelled off nicely towards the surrounding hills and valleys. That's what I'll do, he thought. Have a run. And try and put my mind at rest for an hour. By the time I do that, then have a shower, tart myself up and have a feed, it'll be time to bundy on at the fabulous Double L Dumpmaster for four hours of dance music no one's allowed to dance to. I can't wait. Les walked back to his room, changed into his training gear, did a few stretches on the balcony then wrapped a sweatband round his head and set off.

The heat had gone out of the day and the run was quite enjoyable. Past a bowling club at the bottom of the hill, traffic was almost non-existent so Les was able to run in the middle of the road and avoid any loose rocks along the side where he could have rolled an ankle. Jogging steadily along Les noticed the surrounding countryside consisted of lush meadows and farms on one side and steep mountains hidden beneath dense forest on the right. He didn't dwell on the Double L Ranch. But he was looking forward to catching up with Eddie tomorrow night. Before Les knew it, he'd burned up half-an-hour going one way and it was time to turn around.

Back at the hotel, Les had a shower and a shave, then flopped on his bunk and read for a while before getting changed, to have something to eat prior to hitting the Double L Ranch. The blue check shirt he wore to the wedding wasn't too crushed. Les put that on over his jeans and a plain blue T-shirt. There was no mirror in the room, but Les felt he looked good enough to spend four hours playing disco duck in a glorified shearing shed. He gave his hair a quick flick and left the hotel.

At the pizza shop, Les ordered a chicken schnitzel with chips and salad then sat down in the restaurant at the same table as the night before. Coincidentally, the same European family as the night before were seated at the same table next to him, hogging into the same pizzas and the same size bottles of Coke. There were half-a-dozen or so other diners in the restaurant, but Les didn't see any bags of pot or notice anyone going out for a toke. His chicken schnitzel arrived and it was very good, not over crumbed, the chips were crisp and the salad was fresh. Les washed it all down with a flat white, lingered to the last, then paid his bill. Before he left the pizza shop, he bought two bottles of mineral water and took them back to his room. Satisfied everything was in order, Les exited the hotel once more and strolled down to the Double L Ranch.

Even with the outside lights on the venue still looked pretty dismal sitting between the two vacant blocks. Standing in front of the double doors were two solid young blokes with square jaws and thick necks both wearing dark blue polo shirts with the Double L logo on the front pocket. One had chunked-up black hair, the other had brown hair combed straight back off his forehead. They stopped talking and gave Les a bit of a once-up-and-down as they watched him coming up the path.

'G'day,' said Les, stopping in front of the two men. 'You must be Mason and Buddy.'

'That's right,' replied the bloke with black hair.

'I'm Les. Your swingin groovin DJ for the next two nights.'

Both men's eyes lit up. 'Hey. How are you, Les?' smiled the bloke with black hair. 'Lonnie told us to expect you. I'm Buddy.'

'G'day, Buddy.' Les shook Buddy's hand.

'And I'm Mason,' said the man with brown hair.

'How are you, Mason?' Les also shook Mason's hand.

'Jesus. I got to say,' said Buddy, 'you don't look much like a DJ, Les.'

'No,' agreed Mason. 'We were expecting some skinny eccyhead dressed in black with a cap on back the front.'

'That's Skunk Daddy,' said Les. 'He starts next week.'

Les had a quick mag to the two doormen. They both came from Lismore and played football. Buddy was a mechanic. Mason built security grilles. Les said he did security work in Sydney and was a friend of a friend of Lonnie's.

'Has Lonnie told you about this no dancing rattle?' asked Les.

Buddy tapped the side of his forehead. 'Yeah. It's got me fucked.'

'Fuckin weird,' said Mason.

'That's what I reckon,' agreed Les. 'Anyway, we'll see what happens.' He glanced at his watch and moved towards the door. 'Okay. I'd better get inside and do my thing. Or Lonnie'll dock my wages. I'll see you before the night's out, fellahs.'

'Righto, Les,' smiled Buddy.

'Have a good one,' said Mason, pushing open the door.

Les stepped into the foyer. It was empty so he walked straight through the archway into the club.

The soft lighting wasn't meant to be soft or set any mood. It was just poorly set up. There were about twenty people seated or standing around and another four at the bar getting served. The three girls were standing behind it pouring or handing out drinks. Les tipped Lonnie would be in his office. He said hello to the girls then lifted up the gate on the bar and stepped into the office. Lonnie was seated in his swivel chair wearing the same polo shirt and jeans.

'Hey, Les. How are you, mate?' smiled Lonnie. 'Right on time too,' he added, glancing up at the clock.

'Well, Lonnie. Eddie warned me you were a tough boss. So I thought I'd better do the right thing.'

'Yeah, right,' chuckled Lonnie.

Les folded his arms across his chest. 'Eddie tells me you and him are mates from Vietnam,' said Les.

'Yeah. I was an Air Force Perimeter Guard. We used to get on the piss together in Saigon.'

'So where are you from, Lonnie, if you don't mind me asking?' said Les.

'Sydney. I grew up in Five Dock.'

'Do you know George Brennan, from the club?'

'George,' smiled Lonnie. 'Reckon. We used to play touch football with the Five Dock Floggers. He wasn't the fastest on the paddock. But get him on a dancefloor, he makes MC Hammer look like he's stuck in quicksand.'

'So I believe,' smiled Les. He looked up at the clock. 'Well, I'd better go and do my thing.'

'Okay. Everything's set up over there. I'll hit the dimmer. All you got to do is play the tracks I've noted. And remember …'

'No dancing,' replied Les.

'Right on, dude. Oh. And if you want a drink, just help yourself.'

'Thanks.'

'And before you start, say hello to Amy in the snack bar. Jock's out there somewhere. Say hello to him too.'

'I'll do that.'

Les left the office and told Kerrie he was going to get a bottle of mineral water. No problem, Les. Go for your life. With his bottle of water Les stepped from behind the bar and walked round to the snack bar. Standing behind the counter wearing jeans and a white T-shirt under a white apron was a dumpy auburn-haired girl with her long hair parted in the middle and held back by a red polkadot bandana. She had nice white teeth and a homely face and could be classed as attractive, except she was violently cross-eyed. She looked up at Les and no matter how hard he tried, Les couldn't tell who or what she was looking at.

'Hello,' smiled Les. 'Are you Amy?'

'That's right,' smiled Amy.

'I'm Les. The DJ. Lonnie said to say hello.'

'Oh. How are you, Les?' Amy's eyes might not have been the best, but she had a lovely smile.

'I'm good,' Les smiled back. 'How are you?'

'I'm good too.'

An overweight young bloke wearing jeans and the same blue polo shirt appeared on Norton's left holding a plastic bucket. He had curly black hair and a full face marked with acne.

'Hey, Amy,' the bloke said quietly. 'Can I have a pie?'

'Sure, Jock,' replied Amy. 'Sauce?'

'Yeah. Give me the bottle.'

'G'day, Jock,' smiled Les, offering his hand. 'I'm Les. The DJ.'

'Ohh. How are you, Les,' replied Jock, shaking Norton's hand.

'Pretty good, mate.' Les gestured to Amy who was taking a pie out of the oven. 'I'll see you later, Amy,' he called out. 'I got to start work.'

'Okay, Les,' she replied, with a cross-eyed smile. 'I'll see you later.'

'See you, Jock.'

'Yeah. See you, Les.'

Les walked over to the DJ booth and let himself in as Lonnie dimmed the lights from the office. While he was getting his bearings he checked out the punters, who were in turn checking out the DJ. They were all clean and reasonably well dressed and well over eighteen. A few more women than men, wearing denim or frilly dresses with coloured ribbons and such in their hair, and although Les couldn't see any beauty queens, none of them had been hit with an ugly stick either. The men looked much the same, mostly wearing jeans and T-shirts with the odd badly ironed shirt tucked in here and there. It was too early for anyone to be drunk. But if the eyes on two couples seated near the DJ booth were any indication, a fair bit of pot had been smoked before some of the punters hit Nimbin's newest nightspot. After a mouthful of mineral water, Les placed the bottle next to the amplifier and adjusted the lamp, then idly flicked through the CDs before picking one out at random: Lucy De Soto and the Handsome Devils' *Whisky Dance*. I wonder who the fuck this is, he thought, looking at the cover. Never bloody heard of them. Lonnie's marked a few tracks. I'll play this one, 'Bullfrog'. In memory of Fabio. Les placed the CD in the player, tuned the track and pressed Play. Oh well, he shrugged. Here we go. Doof-doof-fuckin-doof. A couple of seconds later, Les nearly fell out of the DJ booth.

It was one of the filthiest rock 'n roll tracks Les had come across in yonks. Twanging steel guitars, hot harmonicas, a thumping bass and other sweet sounds came howling out of the Bose speakers, pushed on by a back beat solid enough to knock down a door. Besides that, the woman singing had a crackling nasally voice that fired the track along like there was no tomorrow. The punters were taken by surprise also. After expecting to be saturated with the same old same old house music, it was a deep breath of fresh rock 'n roll air. As soon as they got over their initial shock, they started banging their heads around, clapping their hands and shaking their shoulders to what was belting out of the bar's A1 sound system.

Les picked out another CD, checked the track and placed it in the player. Then as soon as 'Bullfrog' finished, the Joe Galea Band started hoofing into 'Do You Have A Garter Belt'. It too was a hot rock 'n roll number. Les followed up with Rock This House — B.B. King and Elton John. Sadie Green — 'Dig T. Tyler'. 'Tuxedo Junction' — Jools Holland and a heap of other kick arse rock 'n roll tracks Norton had never heard before.

More punters drifted in till the place was over half full. Jock kept Les supplied with cold mineral water, Buddy and Mason came in to make sure everything was okay, while the time flew. And I thought I was going to be stuck playing house music, laughed Les, as 'Madison Blues' — George Thorogood finished and he played Shooter Jennings' hot version of the old Dire Straits number 'Walk of Life'. This is rock 'n roll heaven.

Then the first hiccup occurred. Flicking through the CDs, Les found *Last Man Standing* — Jerry Lee Lewis. And Lonnie had marked 'Hadacol Boogie'. The first four bars hadn't pumped out of the speakers when two beefy blondes wearing black denim and their hair braided got up and started dancing. Well. Here goes nothing, thought Les and flicked the yellow switch. The NO DANCING sign started flashing on and off and from out of nowhere, Lonnie came running over.

'What do you think you're doing?' he yelled at the two beefy blondes.

'We're dancing. What does it fuckin look like?' the beefiest of the two blondes yelled back.

'Well, stop it,' said Lonnie. 'Or I'll have you thrown out.'

'What?' said her girlfriend.

Lonnie pointed to the flashing red sign. 'There's no dancefloor. And them's the rules. And if you don't like it you can leave.'

'You're off your fuckin head, sport,' said the first blonde.

'Maybe,' replied Lonnie. 'But I own the place. So sit down and behave yourself. Or you're out the door.'

'I don't fuckin believe it,' said her girlfriend.

The girls sat down, Lonnie returned to the bar and Les switched the sign off. Then the girls started glaring at Les. He got another track ready when the beefiest blonde rose to her feet, pulled her jeans up round her fat arse then came marching through the punters over to the DJ booth and climbed the stairs.

'Hey, you,' she called out.

'Yes. Can I help you, miss?' smiled Les.

'Yeah,' scowled the blonde. 'What's all this no dancing shit?'

'I don't know,' shrugged Les. 'I'm just working here trying to pay off a mortgage.'

'Well, it's pretty fucked if you ask me.'

'Maybe,' said Les. 'But there's a sign on the front of the booth letting you know. You got a beef. Go see the boss.'

'Fuck you,' cursed the blonde.

Les gave her an impassive once-up-and-down. 'You wouldn't say that if my wife was here.'

'Cunt.'

'I don't know if we've got that,' smiled Les. 'Who sings it?'

The blonde stormed off and rejoined her girlfriend glaring at Les. Les had a drink of mineral water and played 'Greasy Kid Stuff' — Kid Ramos.

After that, the punters got more drink and hot ones into them and things got worse. People kept getting up and dancing, Les kept pushing the yellow button and Lonnie kept running over and stopping them, then they'd come up and abuse Les. One tall wiry bloke with a black mullet and tattoos wearing jeans and an old green flannelette shirt got told three times to stop dancing. He had a couple of goes at Les and towards the end of the night, Lonnie came over with Buddy and Mason and threw the bloke and his three mates out. Watching from the DJ booth, Les was impressed with the way the two doormen managed to do it without any spilled drinks, spilled blood or unnecessary drama. Les finished another bottle of mineral water, looked at his watch and couldn't believe how fast the night had gone. It was time for the last track. He fished up 'Juicy Fruit' — Rudy Green and when it was over put the CD back with the others then stood there looking out at the crowd who were giving him mixed looks; some thought he was a hero for playing all that good music; most thought he was an absolute dropkick for stopping them from enjoying themselves. Les was hoping he'd make it out of the club without getting his clothes torn off when the lights came on and Lonnie appeared at the entrance to the DJ's booth.

'So how did your gala opening night go, Lonnie?' asked Les.

'About what I expected,' replied Lonnie. 'How was it for you?'

'How was it for me?' echoed Les. 'Well, I did what you asked. And when I wasn't getting abused by everyone, it was great. The last time I heard music as good as that was at a blues festival down the south coast.'

'Not bad rock 'n roll eh?'

'Fantastic. But I'm playing all that grouse music,' complained Les, 'yet at the same time I've got to make a complete twenty-four carat dropkick of myself and push the No Dancing switch when the punters do no more than start having a good time. Fair dinkum, Lonnie. You can't be playing with a full deck.'

'I know. It's a funny one,' smiled Lonnie.

'And you'll explain it all to me tomorrow night, when Eddie gets here.'

'Exactemondo, hombre.'

'All right,' shrugged Les. 'So where did you get all those CDs, anyway? Most of them, I've never heard of.'

'Off a sheila in Bondi,' answered Lonnie.

'Not Side Valve Susie, by any chance?'

'Yeah. You know her?'

'I sure do. She's an old friend of mine. Lives just down the road.'

'She's getting me some more,' said Lonnie. 'She's a genius. You just tell her what you want, and she'll have it for you in a week. At a good price, too.'

'That's Susie,' nodded Les.

'So what are you doing now, Les?' Lonnie asked. 'You want to stay back and have a few staffies? You can't drink mineral water all night. People'll think you're a poof.'

Les thought for a moment. 'To be honest, Lonnie, I gave the piss a bit of a nudge last night. I might drag my sorry arse back to the hotel and go straight to bed. Give my ears a rest. Maybe tomorrow night when I catch up with Eddie.'

'Fair enough.'

'Will you say goodnight to the girls and that for me?'

'Yeah. No worries. We'll be doing the tills and fucking around here for a while yet.'

'All right,' said Les, moving towards the stairs. 'Well, I'll just exit stage right and be on my way.'

'Okay, Les,' winked Lonnie. 'I'll see you tomorrow night at eight.'

'Righto, Lonnie. See you then.'

Buddy and Mason were slowly moving the remaining punters out of the room as Les eased his way through. He gave the boys a wink and said he'd see them tomorrow night. They smiled back and Les left the bar. Outside the people drifting around in the dark didn't notice him, so Les turned left for the short walk back to his room.

Well, isn't life full of surprises, mused Les as he came to the start of the hill leading up towards the hotel. I thought I was going to be punished unmercifully with house music. Instead, that was a blast. Ronnie sure knows a good rock track or two. Bad luck he's dirty on people dancing, though. The joint would have gone off. Anyway. It's on again tomorrow night. Right now I just want to put my head down. Les had just reached the hotel when four figures appeared, coming across the road from the war memorial.

'Hey. Fuckin you,' one of the figures called out in a voice filled with drunken belligerence.

Les turned around to find the bloke with the mullet who had got thrown out of the club coming towards him with his three mates. They were all dressed much the same in black T-shirts and jeans and looked much the same, except for one who had a ginger buzz cut.

'Oh shit,' said Les. 'What do you want?'

'You got us thrown out of the bar tonight, you cunt,' said the bloke with the mullet.

'Mate,' said Les. 'I didn't get you thrown out. You got yourselves thrown out. To be honest, I reckon that No Dancing rattle is a pretty stupid idea. But I got to do what the boss tells me.'

'Ohh, bullshit,' said one of Mullet's mates, wearing a Guns N' Roses T-shirt. 'You're just a fuckin nark.'

'Yeah, whatever,' replied Les.

'You fucked up our night,' said Mullet. 'We were getting onto some chicks in there, till you put your fuckin head in.'

'Well, come back tomorrow night,' said Les. 'I'm sure there'll be plenty more girls there absolutely fanging to meet four studs like you.'

'You're a fuckin smartarse, mate,' said one of Mullet's pals.

'Whatever you say,' replied Les. 'Now if you'll excuse me, gents, I'm going to bed. Goodnight.'

Les started climbing the stairs when one of the group yelled out, 'Go on. Get the cunt, Raggsie.'

Les turned around to find the bloke with the mullet clambering up the stairs behind him while the others waited at the bottom. Norton waited till the bloke was two steps below him, then brought his right leg back and punt-kicked him under the chin. Raggsie let out a howl of pain and tumbled back down the stairs into his mates. He was lying on his back across the footpath when Les came flying off the stairs and landed heels first into the bloke's stomach, rupturing his sternum. Raggsie's mouth opened, there was a brief gagging sound, then his eyes rolled back and he lay there motionless. Les jumped off him and planted two left hooks into the closest face he could find, splitting whoever it belonged to's mouth open and sitting him on his backside. The bloke had barely fallen, when Les drew his right foot back and snap-kicked the next bloke in the groin, doubling him over. His eyes bulged agonisingly at Les, before Norton dropped him with a lightning fast crescent-kick to the jaw. This left Buzz Cut standing on his own and not the slightest bit interested in mixing it with the DJ.

'Come on, shithead,' gestured Les. 'What do you want to do?'

Buzz Cut retreated to the laneway and tried to look tough. He poked out his chin and pointed at Les. 'You're dead meat, mate. We know where you live. And we'll fuckin get you.'

'Yeah?' replied Les. 'I've heard that before.' Les quickly advanced along the footpath towards Buzz

Cut. But Buzz Cut had already figured discretion was the better part of valour. He turned and fled and was past the Hemp Embassy picking up speed when Les yelled out, 'Yeah, go on. Fuck off. You little turd.' Les turned back, stopping for a moment to have a last look at the three blokes lying moaning and bleeding on the footpath, before he started up the stairs.

'Now,' he said cordially. 'If you fine fellows will excuse me, I'd like to go to bed. The night has been unusual, to say the least. Good evening, gentlemen.' Les let himself in the front door then took the stairs to the corridor and went straight to the bathroom.

Back in his room, Les closed the door behind him, climbed out of his clothes and laid them on the top bunk next to his bags. Oh yes, he smiled, standing in his jox. How sweet it is. No stinking of cigarette smoke. Thank you. Yawning now, Les climbed into his trackies, had a long drink of water then folded up the same black T-shirt, turned off the light and climbed into his bunk. He wrapped the T-shirt across his eyes, yawned, took in a deep breath through his nose and relaxed. He started to think about the night at the club, the fight out the front and Lonnie's eccentricity. Before long Les figured there was nothing worth thinking about. It was all too weird. Another yawn, a scrunch of his head into the pillows and soon Norton was snoring soundly.

After a good night's sleep, Les woke up reasonably early the next morning feeling fresh as a daisy. He gazed around the room for a moment, then climbed out of his bunk, got his towel and shaving kit and, not having any sign of a hangover to contend with, cheerfully strode off down the corridor to the bathroom. When he'd finished, Les returned to his room, opened the back door and, still in his trackies, stepped out onto the verandah to see what the day was doing.

It was much the same as Friday, mild and sunny, with patches of fat clouds drifting along in the breeze and no sign of rain. In the street below, Nimbin was still barely coming to life. Apart from the odd vehicle driving past, the only signs of movement were a few people coming and going at the newsagency across the road. Les had a stretch then strolled down to the far end of the verandah to view the mist rising from the hills and valleys while he took a few deep breaths. Hello, smiled

Les, when he stopped at the end railing, looks like the old French bloke's back in the hood. What's the old troublemaker and his wife up to this time?

Parked on its own next to the war memorial was the white Winnebago with the tricolour flag in the rear window. Les watched as the driver's door opened and the old bloke got out, wearing a light green tracksuit, a khaki giggle hat and a big pair of sunglasses. Gripped firmly in his right hand was an aluminium walking stick. The old bloke closed the door then hobbled slowly across the road, his attention fixed on something near the Hemp Embassy. Les moved across to the long railing, poked his head over the side and had a look.

Strolling casually across the laneway on his own was the dealer the others called Ray; the one who had abused the old bloke the previous afternoon. Well, what do you know, mused Les, picking up on the dark blue tracksuit with the red piping. It's our friendly neighbourhood dope dealer. Probably getting ready to meet the other sales reps for a power breakfast while they work out their sales plan for the day. Ray continued walking beneath the verandah, towards the driveway that separated the hotel from the shops next door. Les watched him for a moment then moved back to the end railing as the old bloke stepped up onto the footpath. From his vantage point by the railing, Les had the same excellent view and again any sounds from the street drifted up loud and clear.

'Excuse me, sir,' the old bloke said to Ray as the man in the blue tracksuit drew near. 'Have you a moment?'

Ray stopped in front of the old bloke leaning on his walking stick and didn't recognise him beneath the hat and sunglasses. 'Yeah. What do you want?' Ray answered curtly.

'My son asked for me to get him weed,' smiled the old bloke. 'You can help, please. Yes?'

'Sure,' replied Ray cordially, the sniff of an easy sale in the air. 'No problems, mate.'

The old bloke indicated the narrow driveway leading to the back of the hotel. 'Do you mind if we go down lane? I am old and nervous. And do not like doing such a thing in open.'

'Good idea,' patronised Ray. 'You can never be too careful.'

'After you, sir.'

'All right,' replied Ray.

They had walked a few short metres down the lane when unexpectedly the old bloke swung his walking stick back like a baseball bat and slammed it against the side of Ray's left knee, buckling the dealer's leg. From his position by the railing, Les had a perfect view and found himself totally gobsmacked.

'Ohh, Jesus fuckin Christ,' screamed Ray. He clutched at his knee in agony, before falling awkwardly onto his right leg. 'Ohh, you fuckin old cunt,' he roared up at the old bloke.

Saying nothing, the old bloke swung the walking stick again and slammed it against the side of Ray's face, slicing his cheekbone open across to his ear. Ray just had time for another scream of pain before the old bloke swung the walking stick again and hit him in the mouth, ripping open his lips and knocking out several teeth. The dealer made a frantic grab for his face when the old bloke raised his walking stick like an axe and brought it down across Ray's bony head, splitting his scalp open.

After that the old bloke simply laid into Ray with sadistic fury till the dealer was lying in a foetal position on the ground, soaked in blood and whimpering with pain. Then the old bloke stopped, rolled Ray onto his back and kicked his legs apart.

'So, you cheeky fucking black fellow bastard,' he said ominously. 'You wish to fuck my beautiful little granddaughter, do you? With fucking what?'

The old bloke raised his walking stick and slammed it into Ray's groin with such ferocity the handle broke. The pain was so excruciating, the dealer couldn't even scream. He simply lay at the old bloke's feet quivering, his bloodied, battered face frozen in horror at what was happening to him. It was that awful a sight, even Les had to momentarily turn away.

The old bloke gave Ray a few more in the groin then stopped, and with a cruel smile on his face, stood over Ray, who was fast going into shock.

'Now listen to me, bastard,' the old bloke said evenly. 'When peoples ask you what happened, tell them you met old colonel from Spetsnaz. Spetsnaz,' he repeated. 'You got that, bastard?' The old bloke gave Ray a last whack across the ribs then threw the broken walking stick into a grassy ditch running beneath the trees alongside the driveway. After a cursory look around, the old bloke calmly walked back to the Winnebago and, without any sign of a limp, climbed behind the wheel and drove off.

Well, smiled Les, as the Winnebago disappeared out of sight, that's something you don't see every day. He turned to Ray lying in the dirt, his chest heaving and his breath coming in tortured gasps. The dealer was a shattered, bloodied mess; if his dark tracksuit hadn't masked most of the blood, it would have looked even worse. Voices coming from beneath the verandah made Les step across to the long railing and poke his head over. It was Ray's two mates in their dark tracksuits.

'He should be here. I saw him drive off.'

'He might have gone round to Dawn's?'

'No. He said he was coming straight to the pub.'

'Maybe he's in the car park. Sorting things out?'

Following them along the verandah, Les watched Ray's mates walk down to the driveway. They saw Ray lying on the ground, gave a shout and ran over to him.

'Jesus Christ,' said the first man, kneeling down by Ray's side. 'Are you all right, Ray?'

'Fuckin hell,' said his mate. 'What happened?'

'I don't know. Shit. Go and get the car. We'll get him to the hospital.'

'Yeah, right.'

The dealer ran off towards the Hemp Embassy, while his mate carefully rolled Ray over on his back. Besides being covered in deep gashes, Ray's leg was broken, so was his left arm, and who knew what internal injuries he had. The first man looked up and saw Les peering over the balcony.

'Hey,' he yelled. 'Did you see what happened?'

Les shook his head. 'No. I just got out of bed. Looks like he's been hit by a car. I'd better ring the police.'

'Fuck the police,' the man shouted back.

'That's exactly what I reckon,' nodded Les.

Norton left the man still tending to Ray and went back to his room. He had a drink of mineral water then, taking his time, changed out of his trackies and into his blue shorts and the same T-shirt he wore at the club. Satisfied his credit cards and money were tucked safely in his pockets, Les walked back down to the end of the verandah.

Ray's two mates had taken him away leaving several thick patches of blood soaking into the driveway. Les stared at the blood for a few moments, thoughtfully picking at his chin. It's funny, he pondered. One minute that old bloke was limping around on a walking stick. The next minute his limp's gone and he's walking as good as gold. He must be onto some miracle cure. Les went back to his room, locked it, then followed the corridor down to the side entrance and let himself out of the hotel. He took the stairs to the footpath and walked over to the driveway.

Ignoring the spot where Ray had been lying, Les started searching in the ditch beneath the trees, and it didn't take him long to find the old bloke's blood-spattered broken walking stick. Using a sheet of newspaper that had blown down the driveway, Les picked it up and immediately his face burst into a huge grin.

'You sneaky, rotten old bastard,' he laughed out loud.

The walking stick was a length of lead pipe, sprayed with silver frost and fitted with a black rubber stopper at one end. At the other end, a piece of wood had been jammed into the pipe to form a handle, part of which had broken off. Les shook his head in grim admiration. No wonder the old bloke made such a mess of that goose. You could wreck a truck with this. Then Les snapped his fingers as something else occurred to him. The flag on the back window of the Winnebago. It wasn't a vertical blue, white and red French flag. It was a horizontal white, blue and red Russian flag. The old bloke wasn't French. He was Russian. And that word he repeated to poor silly Ray, 'Spetsnaz'. They're the Russian Special Forces. Eddie's showed me videos of them. Shit! They're as tough and hard as any soldiers in the world. The only difference with them is, they're more brutal and utterly ruthless. The old bloke was ex-Spetsnaz. Christ! Ray's lucky he didn't beat him to death. And you can bet if Ray's two mates had been with him, the old warrior wouldn't have hesitated in giving it to them, too. Les balanced the length of pipe in his hand. Well, I'll be buggered. Wait till I tell Eddie about this tonight. He'll blow in his pants. After one more look, Les dumped the length of pipe back in the ditch and walked across to the newsagency.

Les bought the three Sydney papers then strolled down to the Spectrum Café. Noticing Gazza wasn't around he placed the papers on one of the tables out the front, removed all the sections he wasn't interested in and dropped them in the nearest bin. The Spectrum's door was open and when he'd finished Les walked straight in to find half-a-dozen people seated in the café eating or drinking coffee, while Rip Van Winkle and the gang were huddled in the garden, all vibed up and ready to waste another day. Les ordered the same meal as before from the same man behind the counter and sat down at the same table. Same old same old, he mused as he opened *The Australian*. The only things missing so far are those fuckin elves. Les had a suspicious look under his table as the man brought his coffee and cutlery over.

The coffee was good and the food when it arrived was as tasty, with a little extra bacon this time. Les enjoyed the meal then lingered over one of the weekend magazines with another coffee. When he'd finished Les paid the bill, gathered his papers and stood out the front of the restaurant figuring out what to do. Between the tourist buses and people walking around, Nimbin had come to life. But Les wasn't interested in strolling through town taking photos and such. He'd seen and bought all he wanted. Why don't I simply spend the day reading the papers and maybe my book? he asked himself. Then, by the time I contemplate my navel, have a run, iron a dress and have a feed it'll be time to bundy on at Lonnie's palaise de boogie. After buying some apples, oranges and more mineral water at the supermarket, Norton walked across to the hotel.

Back in his room, Les kicked off his trainers and took the papers out onto the verandah. He had settled down at a table near his back door when the smell of someone smoking pot drifted up through the floorboards. A glance over the railing told Les three younger sales reps in tracksuits had taken over the franchise and business appeared to be brisk. There you go, smiled Norton, as he resumed his seat. Ray's certainly got some reliable back-up in his sales team. I wonder how the sales manager's feeling right now? VFO, I would imagine.

By late afternoon, Les had eaten all his fruit, drunk a bottle of mineral water and read every book, film and theatre review imaginable. He'd caught up on news from all over the world and gone through each boring long-winded political column there was, wishing he'd read his book instead. Boy! Do I need a run, he told himself, as he dumped the three papers in a plastic garbage bin down from his door. Between Alan Ramsay, Paul Kelly and the rest of those Canberra hacks, I feel like my brain's turned to boiled choko. He changed into his training gear, did a few stretches on the railing then let himself out of the hotel and jogged off in the same direction as the day before.

Again traffic was almost zero and the run was enjoyable. Les tried to keep a clear head. But pictures of the old bloke hammering the dealer in the blue tracksuit kept going through his mind. What's that old saying? mused Les. Revenge is a dish best served cold. Try telling that to the old Russian in the Winnebago. He preferred shoving it in a microwave oven and leaving it on high for about twenty-five minutes. Les looked at his watch. Jogging nonchalantly along, he'd come a little further than the day before. He turned around and started back.

When Les got to the hotel there was a blue minibus parked out the front with LITTLE RIPPER AUSSIE TOURS painted along the side. And when he let himself into his room, his clothes had been neatly folded and placed on the bunk above his along with his bags and two bulky backpacks. Besides that, the back door was open and he had company.

Lying on the bottom bunk opposite his was a fat blue-eyed blonde with her hair braided into two thick plaits; lying on the bunk above her was an even bigger blonde with her hair parted in the middle. They were both wearing jeans, folded at the bottom, socks and sandals and floppy white T-shirts. Their bling was coloured beads and metal bangles.

'G'day,' said Les, removing his sweatband.

'Hello,' drawled the blonde on the top bunk.

'Hello,' drawled her girlfriend.

Les got a bottle of mineral water, had a drink and sat down on his bunk. The blonde on the top bunk slid her massive behind over the side and sat down next to her friend on the bottom bunk where they both stared at Les staring back at them from about a metre away.

'I'm Les, anyway,' said Norton, offering his hand.

'I am Nissa,' replied the blonde with the plaits, pumping Norton's hand.

'And I am Solveig,' said the other blonde, doing the same.

'Nice to meet you,' smiled Les.

'You also,' smiled Solveig.

'We hope you don't mind we moved your clothes?' said Nissa.

Les shook his head. 'No. That's all right,' he said. Les stared at the two girls and swallowed some more water. 'So what's doing?' he asked.

The girls turned to each other for a moment. 'What's … doing?' asked Nissa.

'Yeah.' Les nodded to the girl's ample breasts. 'How are they hanging? Soft as silk and full of milk. Or fat and dud and full of mud?'

The two girls looked at each other again and exchanged words in a foreign language. Solveig turned to Les and shook her head.

'We do not understand,' she said.

'That's okay,' smiled Les. 'I have a tendency to talk a bit fast. It comes from living in the Eastern Suburbs. So where are you from?'

'From?' said Nissa.

'Yeah. Where's home?' asked Les. 'You're not Poms, are you?' he joked.

'Oh no,' stated Solveig. 'We are not Poms.'

191

It turned out the girls were Norwegian university students from a town called Trondheim, where they studied graphic art. They'd been in Australia for three days: in Sydney. Now they were heading for Fraser Island with ten other backpackers, after a stopover in Nimbin till Monday. Later they were going to Cairns and Darwin. Les told them the truth. He was from Sydney and he was in Nimbin working as a disc jockey, helping a bloke get a bar going. He'd be gone in the morning. The girls' English wasn't too bad in a sing-song fashion. But although Les was talking slowly, they'd often have to turn to each other and discuss something he'd just said in their native Norwegian.

'And you are disc jockey?' queried Solveig.

'Too right,' replied Les. 'I'm one cool rockin hep cat daddy. Why don't you come down the club tonight and check things out? You like rock 'n roll?'

'Rock and roll is good,' replied Solveig.

'Yes,' smiled Nissa. 'I like to boogie on Saturday night.'

'T-Rex,' winked Les. 'Then you'll like the Double L Ranch.'

'Double L Ranch,' drawled Solveig. 'Sounds very good.'

'It is,' said Les. 'Anyway, girls, I have to have a

shower and get ready for the pickle factory. Showbiz and my fans are calling.'

'Whatever you say,' replied Nissa.

Les rose from the bed and, feeling a little self-conscious due to the cramped conditions in the room, gathered up his towel and shaving kit. Shit! This is ridiculous, he frowned. There's not enough room in here to swing a mouse, let alone a cat. Be nice if I rub against Nissa or Solveig while I'm getting changed and Mr Wobbly pokes his head out. Sleeping's going to be a lot of fun, too, if I come home half-pissed after catching up with Eddie.

Les found a clean pair of jox and was about to leave when Solveig raised one cheek of her ample rump from the bunk and ripped off a fart that sounded like somebody tearing an old bedsheet in half. Taking absolutely no notice, Nissa snorted back through her nose, cleared her throat and gobbed out the back door. Well, smiled Les, holding on to his toiletries. I guess that's set the tone for the night. No problems. Les excused himself and just before he stepped out the door, let go a fart that had been crammed inside him while he'd been sitting on his bunk talking. Les closed the door softly behind him and, whistling happily, strolled down to the showers.

When he got back to the room, Nissa and Solveig were seated out on the verandah stuffing themselves with corn chips and drinking orange juice. Les changed into his jeans and a dark blue denim shirt that was only crushed at the back, over a black souvenir T-shirt he bought in Lorne. After giving his hair a brief flick, he stepped out onto the verandah and joined the two Norwegians by their table.

'Oh. Have a look at you,' said Solveig.

'Yes. You are very handsome man, Les,' smiled Nissa. 'I bet girls go crazy for you in disco.'

Les had a strong feeling the Norwegian girls were being just a little sarcastic, because he'd had a good look at his face while he was shaving, and Brad Pitt he wasn't. But Les didn't mind a bit of friendly banter. 'You better believe it, barge arse,' he winked. 'As soon as I walk in the door, I'll have snatches hurled at me like javelins.'

'Snatches like javelins?' queried Solveig.

'Yeah. Big ones, little ones. Hairy ones, smelly ones. I might even get a whopper like yours, and have to lash a couple of fence palings across my back so I don't fall in.'

Nissa tilted her head a little. 'You know,' she half smiled, 'I think you are very cheeky man, Les.'

'Yes. Very cheeky for sure,' agreed Solveig.

'Me?' protested Les. 'No way camel-toe ted. I was brought up in a very strict family of God-fearing Christians.'

Nissa turned to Solveig and they had a quick exchange in their native tongue. 'You know anything about Norwegian women, Les?' asked Nissa.

'Yeah. I used to take a Norwegian girl out in Sydney. She drove a fjord fijalcon.'

Solveig ignored Les and stared directly into his eyes. 'Maybe when you finish tonight at disco,' she said, 'we have party back here. Nissa has bottle of Norwegian aquavit in bag.' Solveig wiggled her eyebrows. 'Is very good, Les. Little bit aniseed. Make you feel hot inside, like big log in fire.'

'Sounds great,' smiled Les. 'I'll try and get away early.' He looked at his watch and moved towards the door. 'Anyway, ladies, I'm off to have something to eat. By then it'll be time to start work. So I'll see you later. You two little Norwegian sweet potatoes.'

'Okay,' nodded Nissa. 'We find you in disco.'

'Yes. Maybe we do that for sure,' said Solveig.

Lord have mercy, shuddered Les as he let himself out of the room and took the stairs to the front door. That's all I need. Come home tonight and have those two mastodons throw me up in the air. I'd rather get into another fight. Fuck it, thought

Les, as he crossed the road to the pizza shop. I'm half a mind to keep off the piss again tonight, get my stuff and drive straight to Ballina when I finish. I noticed an all-night motel there as I was driving in. I can stay there tonight and get a fresh start in the morning. Shit. I might just do that. I can always have a drink with Eddie in Sydney.

Les went for the chicken schnitzel again, plus a smoked salmon salad and a flat white to wash everything down. The dining room was half full and Les found a table beneath the paintings where he settled back to check out the other diners. They were mostly families, except for a table of four girls near the window, who kept glancing in his direction over their glasses of white wine. Les surmised they had been at the bar the night before and recognised the nark DJ that wouldn't let anyone dance.

Having not eaten anything except fruit since breakfast, Les had no trouble knocking over both the salmon salad and the schnitzel, along with a second flat white. Fair dinkum, thought Les, as he drained the last of his second coffee, wouldn't it be nice right now to be home on my lounge, kicked back in my trackies, catching up with Alan, Charlie and Jake in *Two and a Half Men*. Still, it could be worse. At least I'm getting to hear some good music.

And five hundred bucks a night's not a bad earn. Les paid the bill and strolled down to the bar.

Several people were drifting in and Buddy and Mason were on the door, looking fit in their polo shirts and jeans when Les came up the path. As soon as they spotted him their faces lit up.

'Les. How are you, mate?' said Buddy.

'Hello, Les. How's things?' asked Mason.

'Not bad, fellahs,' smiled Les. 'How's it with you?'

'Good,' smiled Mason.

'Hey, Les,' said Buddy. 'Did you get into a fight outside the hotel last night?'

'Yeah,' nodded Les. 'With that bloke and his three mates you threw out.'

'Apparently you didn't do a bad job on them,' said Mason.

'Yeah,' shrugged Norton. 'A couple of them forgot to duck. How did you know?'

'Jock told us,' answered Mason. 'He knows them from round here.'

'There's talk about getting you tonight after work,' said Buddy.

'Yes. One of the heroes mumbled something about that as he was running away.'

'It might be an idea if we walk you back to the hotel when you finish,' suggested Buddy.

'Okay,' nodded Les. 'That'd be good, Buddy. Thanks.'

'No problem at all, Les.'

'So how's Lonnie tonight?' asked Les.

'Ohh, don't even ask,' replied Mason. 'He's got the shits good and proper.'

'Yes. He is not a happy man,' added Buddy.

'What's up?' said Les.

'Dunno,' said Mason. 'He didn't say. But something's on his mind.'

'Well. Whatever it is,' said Les, 'I'd better go inside and do my thing. I'll catch up with you before the night's over.'

'For sure, Les.' Buddy opened the door and Les stepped into the foyer.

As usual, the foyer was empty. But the room was almost half full. The girls were busy behind the bar and Jock was out on the floor with a bucket picking up glasses and bottles. Les gave the girls a wave then stepped under the bar gate before walking into the office. Lonnie was in his office chair, staring into thin air with a worried look on his face.

'G'day, Lonnie,' smiled Les. 'How's things?'

Lonnie looked up, but didn't return Norton's smile. 'How's things?' he repeated. 'Up to shit.'

'Why? What's wrong?' asked Les.

'Eddie ain't going to be here.'

'He's not? Why? What's up?'

'Did you know he had a crook ankle?' said Lonnie.

'Yeah,' nodded Les. 'He sprained it playing squash with George Brennan.'

'Well, George fell on it and nearly broke it.'

'George fell on it?' Les was astounded.

'Yeah. Coming out of a restaurant last night. Now Eddie's ankle's in plaster and he's on crutches. He rang me this morning.'

'Shit!' exclaimed Les. 'So does this make much difference to you?'

Lonnie stared grimly up at Les. 'Does it make much difference? Yeah. Just a fuckin bit.'

Les didn't quite know what to say. 'Is there anything I can do?' he offered.

Lonnie gave a tiny shrug. 'No. Not really, I don't suppose. Just go out there and play the music.'

'Righto.'

'Hey, I heard you got into a fight last night,' said Lonnie.

'Yeah,' nodded Les. 'Outside the hotel.'

'Jock reckons there's a team coming back to get you.'

'That's what Buddy and Mason said too. They're going to hold my hand and walk me home.'

Lonnie shook his head. 'Fuck. It never rains but it fuckin pours.'

'So they say.' Les glanced up at the clock. 'Well. I'd better go and do my thing. I imagine I'll see you as the night progresses, Lonnie.'

'Undoubtedly, Les,' replied Lonnie. 'Un-fuckin-doubtedly.'

Les left Lonnie in his office and got two bottles of mineral water before walking across to the DJ's booth. Shit. What a bummer, scowled Les as he opened the half door and stepped inside. No Eddie. Which means I now put plan B into action. Stay off the piss and get my gear out of the pub. Tell Frau Schmidt and her fat mate to get rooted, then split for that all-night motel in Ballina. And with a little bit of luck and the creek don't rise, I'll be home tomorrow night with a thousand bucks in my kick and all this shit behind me.

Les gazed out over the punters who were giving him mixed looks. Okay. What am I going to play first up for these fuckin hillbillies? Les had a drink of water, closed his eyes then fished out a CD and checked the back. This'll do, smiled Les. Bob Dylan — 'Thunder on the Mountain'. Les put the CD in the player, cued the track and pressed play. Seconds later, more good rock 'n roll came pumping out of the speakers.

Les followed this with 'Pennsylvania six–5000' — Brian Setzer. 'Break Up' — Johnny Green's Blues Cowboys. 'Solid Gold' — Eagles of Death Metal. 'Hep Cat Roar' — Pete Cornelius and the Devilles. And 'Uncommon Connection' — John Hiatt. Before long the place was filling up, Lonnie and the girls were flat out behind the bar and the punters were starting to get restless. Jock came over and asked Les if he wanted any mineral water.

'Yeah. You may as well get me another couple of bottles,' replied Les. 'It's starting to get a bit hot in here. Get me some ice too, will you?'

'Sure. No problem, Les,' said Jock.

'Hey, Jock,' said Les. 'Buddy and Mason told me you reckon those blokes I had a stink with last night, their mates might be waiting for me outside the hotel later.'

'That's what I heard,' replied Jock. 'They're all rugby union players. And they're not real happy about what happened.'

Les flashed onto the length of lead pipe lying in the laneway. 'They might be in for a bit of a surprise,' he smiled.

'I'm sure they will,' nodded Jock. He was about to walk off when he stopped and turned to Les. 'Hey, Les,' he said. 'Do you mind if I ask you something?'

'No. Go for your life, Jock.'

'Are you some kind of ninja superman or something?'

'Why's that?' laughed Les.

'Well, I know Raggsie, one of the blokes you belted. And he's a good footy player and not a bad fighter.'

'So?' shrugged Les.

'Well now he's in hospital with four broken ribs, a busted sternum and a ruptured spleen. Roy Holland's got a broken jaw. And Fritz had to get twelve stitches in his mouth and four teeth put back in.'

Les placed his hand on Jock's shoulder. 'Let's just say they all landed awkwardly.'

'I'll go and get you your mineral water,' said Jock.

'Thanks, mate.'

'Rock Everybody Rock' — McKinley Mitchell cut out and Les played 'Good Rockin' Tonight' — Lucy De Soto. But the one that got the punters going was 'Boogie Woogie Country Girl' — Roomful of Blues. The first tinkles of honky tonk piano bopped out of the speakers and six punters jumped up and started going for it. Les flicked the No Dancing switch and in no time Lonnie came flying over and ordered them to settle down.

After that it was chaos. Les kept finding more good rock 'n roll tracks, more people got up and started dancing, Les flicked the yellow switch and Lonnie would race over and tell everybody to settle down or they were out. After getting abused by three blondes, two brunettes, a redhead and a beefy bloke with tattooed arms, Les was starting to get the shits. He put on 'Hula Hoop' — Anson Funderburgh and was taking a drink of water when he noticed a dark-haired man wearing a blue suit and a brown-haired man with a moustache, wearing a grey suit, come through the archway and start looking po-faced around the room.

What's the betting, thought Les as he placed another CD in the player, they're the licensing police. You couldn't put enough money on it. The two men walked across to the bar, Lonnie caught their eye and did his best to smile before taking them into his office. Before too long, they all came out of the office and Lonnie led the two men across to the DJ booth. The two men looked up at Les, Les gave them a smile and got a curt nod in return before Lonnie pointed out the No Dancing sign on the front of the booth to them.

'Hey, Les,' he called out. 'Hit the yellow switch.'

Les flicked the yellow switch and the No Dancing sign between the windows flashed on and off.

Lonnie and the two men in suits went into a huddle and before long the two men stood looking at each other somewhat nonplussed. Next thing Lonnie was escorting them to the front door and they were gone. Shortly after, Lonnie returned to the DJ's booth.

'That was the licensing police,' he said.

'I thought they might have been,' replied Les. 'How did everything go?'

'Not bad,' nodded Lonnie, attempting another smile. 'Not bad at all.'

'Good,' said Les. 'Because I want to have a word with you.'

'Oh? What's up?' asked Lonnie.

'What's up?' echoed Les. Les flicked the yellow switch and the No Dancing sign flashed on and off. 'That's what's up. That fuckin thing. It's starting to give me the shits.' Les switched it off. 'I've been getting dirty looks and abuse all night. That's the reason I got into a fight with those dills last night. And you can bet I'll get into another one tonight. That's before I get round to the team waiting outside the hotel for me when I go home. So I'll tell you what I'm going to do, Lonnie.'

'Go on,' said Lonnie.

'I'm not switching the fuckin thing on again,' declared Les. 'And if you don't like it, you can get fucked and play your music your fuckin self. And you can stick your thousand bucks in your arse too. Fuck it.' Les gave Lonnie a curt nod. 'There. Now you know.'

Lonnie stared impassively back at Les. 'All right,' he shrugged. 'If they want to dance, let 'em. I've proved my point.' Saying that, Lonnie abruptly turned and walked back to the bar.

Bloody hell. What a weirdo, thought Les as he watched Lonnie walk away. I still don't know what his problem is. But this certainly makes things easier for me. Okay. Now let's have some fun. Les flicked through the CDs and came up with AC/DC — 'Big Jack'. The solid back beat and the mean guitar riff thumped out of the speakers and the punters started moving around on their seats. Picking up a lot of dirty looks, Les gazed out over the crowd and grinned. He raised his arms in the air then made gestures with his hands inviting anybody who wanted to get up and boogie to go for it. To get the ball rolling Norton started hoofing around in the DJ booth. The crowd didn't need to be told twice. Within seconds, those that wanted to were dancing, singing and stomping around the chairs and tables.

After that the night was like one big party. Les played everything from 'Chicken Shack' — Willie

and the Poor Boys to 'Down along the Cove' —
Duke Robillard. He even hit the punters with some
more Lucy De Soto. Then, amongst the racks of
CDs, Les found the Holy Grail of rock music: The
Doors *Other Voices* and The Doors *Full Circle*.
The two albums they recorded after Jim Morrison
died. They were as rare as rocking horse shit. Lonnie
had the original vinyl albums burnt onto CDs and
had marked 'Get Up and Dance' and 'Hardwood
Floor'. Les played both tracks one after the other and
the crowd loved them. But the two tracks that got
the whole place jumping were 'I'm Working On A
Building' — John Fogarty, and 'Circle' — Debi
Candish and Po Boys. Somehow Les played both
songs one after the other and the room almost
turned into an evangelical event. The punters were
singing, dancing, waving their arms and happy
clapping round the room like they were expecting
Jesus himself to walk in the door with John the
Baptist and order two Jack Daniel's and Coke, ice
and slice. Watching the punters having such a good
time and being able to relax, Les was a little sorry
the night would have to end. Then through the
crowd he saw Nissa and Solveig with two
testosterone pumping young studs hanging all over
them and had a fair idea where the boys would

finish up later, so he was happy he'd be finishing before long and high-tailing it out of town. From out of the crowd, Jock appeared at the door to the DJ booth with two cold bottles of mineral water.

'Hey, Jock,' smiled Les, taking the bottles and placing them alongside the amplifier. 'How's it going, mate?'

'Les,' said Jock. 'I got some bad news for you, mate.'

'Yeah? What's wrong?' replied Les.

'Buddy and Mason had a fight out the front. Buddy's busted his wrist and Mason's hurt his knee. So they're going straight to hospital after work for X-rays, and they won't be able to walk you home.'

'Yeah?' said Les. 'Well, it looks like you'll have to back me up, dude.'

Jock shook his head. 'Les,' he said seriously. 'I'm a lover, not a fighter. And I'm not much of a lover either.'

'Don't worry about it, Jock,' smiled Les. 'I'll sort it out.'

'I'm sure you will, Les.'

What did Lonnie say, thought Les, as he watched Jock move back through the crowd with his bucket. It never rains but it pours. He wasn't wrong. But not to worry. I'll just take a detour round those two shops and get the old bloke's walking stick from where I left it in the ditch. The local heroes won't be expecting that. And once I smash the first three or four kneecaps and the rest know I mean business, I reckon they'll soon drop off. Better still, I should be able to sneak in the back door without them knowing. That'll save a lot of aggro and my arse as well, in case the walking stick isn't there. By the time the mugs figure out I'm gone, I'll be halfway to Ballina.

Les played 'Sonic Boom' — Guitar Shorty, and 'Long Time Dead' — Jack Rabbit Slim. And before he knew it, it was time for the last track. Les flicked through the CDs and found the only single amongst them: 'Rock DJ' — Robbie Williams. Oh yes, smiled Norton. It's a bit disco, but I like this. Les slipped it on and watched the punters go for their lives. They danced, they grooved, they sang the lyrics. Next thing it was all over. The lights came on and Les stood back with his bottle of mineral water. Suddenly the crowd turned towards the DJ booth and gave Norton a standing ovation. Taken by surprise after all the previous aggro, Les grinned sheepishly and took a bow. The two beefy blondes from the night before came up and drunkenly said it was one of the best nights they'd had. And it was a good idea he'd fucked off that No Dancing sign or they would have wrapped it round his head. Les thanked them with a kiss on the cheek and said he agreed wholeheartedly. Then a skinny hippy in a red kaftan came up to the DJ booth. He had long black hair with a leather band round it and could have passed for Neil out of *The Young Ones*.

'Hey, man,' he said in a flat whiney voice. 'That music was freaking unreal, man. I mean. Like, you know. It was such a cool vibe, man.'

'Ohh, wow, man,' replied Les. 'I'm like. So glad you dug it, man. Cause for a while there, I was like. You know. Freaked out on a nowheresville groove trip, with all this really heavy shit going down. And then it was like. Just a beautiful scene full of beautiful people. I mean like. Really, really unreal, man.'

'Ohh, yeah, I can dig that, man. I really know where you're coming from. You're out there, man. You're cosmic.'

'Thanks, man. You're a really beautiful person.'

The hippy offered Les his hand and Les had to give him one of those wraparound California handshakes that always made Norton cringe.

'Peace, man,' said the hippy. 'Keep it real, dude.'

'Yeah, man,' replied Les. 'Hang loose, keep cool and fly low.'

Brother, can I find them, thought Les as he watched the hippy rejoin his mates seated near the snack bar, where they finished their last drinks. Buddy and Mason came inside and started moving the remaining punters out the door. Mason limped up to the DJ booth and Les noticed Buddy favouring his left hand.

'Hey, Les,' said Mason. 'Did Jock tell you what happened?'

'Yeah. You and Buddy hurt yourselves out the front and you won't be walking me home,' answered Les.

'We're really sorry, Les. I can just walk and Buddy's hand's fucked. We'd be useless. We'd get someone to help you. But we're not from round here and we don't know anyone.'

'That's all right, Mason,' smiled Les. 'Don't worry about it. I got a secret weapon.'

'All right. But just be careful.'

What a couple of good blokes, thought Les, as he watched Mason limp off and move a few more punters out the door. Good country boys. You can't beat them.

Lonnie suddenly appeared at the gate to the DJ's booth. 'How's things?' he asked.

'All right,' replied Les. 'Once the punters started

dancing, it was like a big party. They even clapped me at the finish.'

'Yeah. I heard them. You know about Buddy and Mason, don't you? They won't be able to walk you home.'

Les nodded. 'It doesn't matter all that much,' he said. 'I can sneak in the back way. And as soon as I get my stuff, I'm heading straight to an all-night motel in Ballina. As well as those idiots waiting out the front, I got two backpackers in my room look like warthogs.'

'Fair enough,' nodded Lonnie. 'See me in the office before you leave. I can run you down the back of the hotel.'

'Okay. That'd be good. Thanks, Lonnie.'

'No worries.' Lonnie turned and walked across to the bar.

Les drummed his fingers on the amplifier. Okay. Now what's my John Dory? He stared across at the snack bar. That's what I'll do. Make myself a cup of coffee. By the time I drink that, Lonnie should have my money sorted out and I can split. Before I make a cup of coffee, I'd better have a piss. I'm busting. Les opened the gate to the DJ booth. Shit, he grimaced as he closed it behind him. I can just imagine what the brasco's going to be like.

Les wasn't wrong. The Gents looked more like a third world rickshaw wash than a toilet. There was water, urine, roaches and vomit from one end to the other, the sink was blocked up and so were the half forty-four gallon drums that formed the urinal, where some smarty had dropped a handful of change on the bottom. Rather than splash his clothes with urine and whatever else, Les pissed on the floor and without even thinking about washing his hands, stepped gingerly out of the toilet and walked across to the snack bar.

There was no sign of Amy, Lonnie appeared to be in his office and the girls were busy on the tills. Norton left them to it and started fossicking around in the snack bar. He found a clean mug and a large can of Golden Roast Instant Coffee. There was hot water in an urn, sugar on the table and milk in the fridge. In no time, Les had a steaming mug of coffee in his hand that didn't taste all that bad. Sitting on top of the fridge were three chocolate biscuits with blue M and Ms on them, left in a plastic bag. Just what I feel like, smiled Les. He helped himself and they went down extra well with his mug of coffee. After he'd finished the last one, Les was wiping a crumb from his mouth when Amy walked into the bar.

'Hello, Amy,' smiled Les. 'How was your night?'

'Fairly busy,' Amy smiled back, her pupils firmly jammed together near the bridge of her nose. 'How about you?'

'Ohh yeah. I kept on rockin. It was good when they all started dancing in the end.'

'Yes. I saw that.' Amy reached on top of the fridge, frowned, and then started running her hands across it. She had another look then turned to Norton. 'Hey, Les,' she asked. 'Did you see a little bag of chocolate biscuits up here?'

'Yeah,' nodded Les. 'I ate them.'

Amy's crossed eyes bulged out of her head like two soft boiled eggs. 'You what?' she said.

'I ate them. I had them with my coffee.'

'Oh my God. You didn't? How could you do that?'

'I don't know,' shrugged Les. 'I just did. Shit I'm sorry, Amy. I suppose I shouldn't have just helped myself. But I'll pay you for them. And the coffee.'

Amy squealed and put her hands over her mouth. 'I'm going to get Lonnie.'

'Hey. There's no need to get the boss, Amy,' reasoned Les. 'I said I'd pay you for them.'

Amy ignored Les and ran out of the snack bar leaving Norton shaking his head. Strike me blue,

213

he thought. Three lousy chocolate biscuits. You'd think I just ate a tin of caviar. Next thing an agitated Amy arrived back at the snack bar with a very concerned Lonnie in tow.

'Did you just eat three of Amy's chocolate biscuits?' demanded Lonnie.

'Yeah,' nodded Les. 'But I apologised and I offered to pay for them. Shit, how much do you want, Amy?' Les patted at his pockets. 'Ten? Twenty dollars? How much is half a packet of chocolate biscuits worth up here?'

Lonnie shook his head. 'You don't understand, Les. They were Nimbin biscuits.'

'Nimbin biscuits?'

'Yeah,' replied Lonnie. 'They were full of dope. Like hash cookies.'

'I bought them to go on a picnic tomorrow with two friends,' explained Amy.

'You did?' said Les.

'Yes. Oh God,' wailed Amy.

'So what's all the big deal?' asked Les. 'I've smoked pot before. Heaps of times.'

'You don't understand, Les,' said Lonnie. 'You've just knocked over something like two hundred joints in one go. In about half-an-hour, you're going to be in orbit.'

'Orbit?'

Lonnie turned to Amy for a second then turned back to Les. Behind Lonnie's eyes, Les could see his mind moving at the speed of sound.

'Right. That's it, Les,' asserted Lonnie. 'You're coming back to my place with me.'

'I am?'

'Yeah. You can't go back to the hotel. You can't drive your car. You're better off at my place.' Lonnie stabbed out a finger. 'Stay where you are. And don't move.'

'Oh, Les,' said Amy. 'What have you done?'

'Had a mug of coffee and some biscuits. That's all,' said Les. 'Shit. What's all the drama? I feel as good as gold.'

'Just stay there, Les,' ordered Lonnie. 'I'll be back in a minute.'

With Amy following, Lonnie left Norton in the snack bar and strode round to the bar. Les still wondered what all the fuss was about. He felt quite normal. Good, actually, considering he'd been on his feet for four hours. Lonnie returned jingling a set of car keys in his hand.

'Okay, Les,' he said. 'Let's get going. Kerrie's going to close up and pay everyone. I'll get us home as quick as I can.'

'Okay,' shrugged Les.

'But before we go, take these.' Lonnie handed Les two white tablets.

'What are these?' asked Les, examining the tablets.

'Mogadons. I brought them in for Kerrie.'

'Sleeping tablets? I don't need sleeping tablets,' protested Les. 'I can sleep under a horse pissing.'

'Believe me, Les,' insisted Lonnie. 'Just take the fuckin things.'

Les shook his head. 'Okay. Anything to make you happy.' Les poured some water into the mug he'd made his coffee in and swallowed the two sleeping tablets. 'There. You satisfied?'

'Yeah. Now come on. Let's go.'

'Whatever you say, Lonnie.'

There was no sign of Amy as Les followed Lonnie around the bar. Mason and Buddy were gone and the girls had finished the tills and were having a staffie. Les gave them a wave and a smile as he went by. The next thing Les knew he was sitting alongside Lonnie in the Colorado and Lonnie had started the engine.

'Hey. Nice car, Lonnie,' said Les, buckling up his seat belt.

'Yeah. I've only had it a few weeks. It goes good.'

Lonnie reversed out of the car park then put his foot down and they sped down the same road and in the same direction Les had jogged along the past two afternoons.

'How far to your place?' asked Les. 'You told me. But I forgot.'

'At this rate,' replied Lonnie, glancing at the speedometer, 'we should be there in twenty minutes.' He looked at Les. 'How are you feeling?'

'Good,' shrugged Les. 'I wouldn't mind another mug of coffee and some more chocolate biscuits.'

'Very funny, Les.'

They had sped past where Norton had jogged to the day before, when a bit further on down the road Les started to feel strange. His eyelids seemed to weigh a kilogram each and his body felt like it weighed a tonne. He turned to Lonnie and found the bar owner had changed. It wasn't an hallucination. Lonnie hadn't turned into something weird similar to when Les had taken magic mushrooms down the south coast. Lonnie had turned into exactly what he was. A carbon-based biped. A moving, breathing pile of flesh and bones with a head on top. Behind the head was a brain and two eyes and beneath all the flesh was a heart, lungs, kidneys and veins, circulating blood through his body loud enough to hear. The car had turned into exactly what it was, too. A big futuristic-looking metal box crammed with lights that glowed in the dark. It had tyres made from rubber that went round in circles and up front was a noisy iron device that exploded petrol pumping into it from a tank under the back. And he was strapped firmly into a seat almost above the tank.

'Oh shit!' murmured Les.

'Are you all right, Les?' asked Lonnie.

'No, I'm not,' answered Les. 'Everything looks different and I feel like I've turned into wet concrete.'

'You're stoned, Les,' said Lonnie. 'Full on. And it's a creeper. It'll keep getting stronger. But don't worry, mate. We'll be home in a few minutes.'

Les was wide-eyed. 'Home?' he said quietly.

'Yeah. My place. So just hang in there, ET. You'll be safe and snoring before you know it.'

'Snoring.' Les chuckled and stared at all the bones in his hands and fingers before gazing out the windscreen at the beautiful night sky. He was gazing away, when suddenly something struck him. It was a revelation. 'Hey, Lonnie,' uttered Les. 'Look at the stars.'

'I know,' replied Lonnie. 'There's a lot of them going around. Anyway. We're nearly there.'

'Where? At the stars?'

'No, Luke Skywalker. My place.'

'Oh,' replied Les, still staring out the windscreen. 'It would be nice if we could go to the stars.'

Completely transfixed, Les continued to stare up at the night sky when Lonnie slowed down and swung the Colorado right at a wooden letterbox almost hidden at the edge of the bush. They lurched over a concrete causeway, then started following a narrow dirt road running between steep hills on the left and level ground on the right thick with trees. They continued on for roughly a kilometre when a rusting metal gate appeared in the headlights. Lonnie stopped the car and got out and unlocked it. He moved the car forward then got out again and locked the gate behind them.

'Is everything all right, Lonnie?' asked Les when Lonnie got back in the car.

'Sort of, Les,' replied Lonnie, putting the Colorado in drive. 'I'll fill you in on everything in the morning.'

'Okay,' smiled Les.

The road climbed for half a kilometre then levelled out onto a clearing with a brown Kingswood station wagon that had seen better days parked on one side. Built above the clearing was a rambling old home with a brick verandah at the front and a covered space underneath. A set of wooden stairs ran up to an entryway on the left with a light on above the door. Lonnie cut the engine and turned to Les.

'Here we are, mate,' he said. 'Home. Are you all right?'

'I don't know,' replied Les. 'I think I am. I'm not sure.'

'Come on. I'll get you to bed.'

'Bed. Yes. That could be good.'

Lonnie helped Les out of the car and Les followed him up the stairs to the front door. Lonnie opened it and they stepped inside into a small foyer next to a loungeroom full of comfortable, if somewhat dated, furniture, along with a good stereo and TV. The verandah Les had noticed was on the right and a hallway with bedrooms and a bathroom on either side led to a kitchen at the back of the house. Les tried to concentrate on the surroundings. But his world had turned into a painting by Vincent Van Gogh: fabulous colours everywhere with a loose sense of perspective.

'Follow me, Les,' said Lonnie.

'Okay, Lonnie,' smiled Les. 'I'll follow you.'

Lonnie led Les to a bedroom on the right and pushed open the door. The room seemed pokey yet large at the same time. There was a window on one side with pastel blue curtains above a single bed covered by a blue duvet and again everything was oozing colours and out of perspective.

'That's a nice, comfortable-looking bed, Lonnie,' said Les.

'And that's where you're going right now, mate,' said Lonnie. 'I want you to get a good night's sleep.'

'Okay,' smiled Les. 'But before I go to bed, Lonnie, just let me show you something.'

'All right. What is it?'

'Take me out to the verandah.'

Lonnie led Les back down the hallway, through the lounge and onto the verandah. Les stared up at the stars, then, feeling like he was Carl Sagan in *Cosmos*, pointed something out to Lonnie.

'Hey, Lonnie. You see the stars,' said Les.

'I do,' replied Lonnie.

'You know why some are brighter than others?'

Lonnie shook his head. 'No, Les. You tell me. Why?'

'Because the brighter ones are closer. And the others are further away. It's not necessarily because they're bigger. It's the distance. In light years.'

Les turned to Lonnie and grinned. 'What do you think of that, Lonnie? Isn't that amazing?'

Lonnie shook his head again, this time in mock admiration. 'You're a deadset genius, Les. They should have you working on the NASA space program.'

'I reckon I could handle that,' agreed Les.

'Come on, Einstein. I'll get you to bed. It's going to be a whole new ball game in the morning.'

'That's all right. I like ball games. Did I tell you I used to play football?' Les went to walk away from the edge of the verandah and found he felt heavier than ever and could hardly move his legs. 'Shit, Lonnie,' he said. 'You might have to help me into bed. I'm gone. I'm so bloody tired too.'

'No worries, mate,' said Lonnie. 'Come on.'

By the time Lonnie got Les onto the bed and out of his trainers, Les not only felt like he was made of lead and living in a Van Gogh painting, but astonishingly tired as well.

'Shit I'm sleepy, Lonnie,' yawned Les. 'I can hardly keep my eyes open.'

'That's the Mogadons kicking in,' said Lonnie, helping Les climb beneath the duvet.

'Mogadons,' smiled Les, sinking his head back onto the pillows. 'Sounds like something out of

Walking with Dinosaurs. Look out. Here comes a herd of Mogadons. We'll all be killed.'

Lonnie gave Norton a pat on the shoulder. 'I'll see you in the morning, Les.'

'Okay,' said Les, closing his eyes.

Lonnie switched the light off and shut the door quietly behind him, leaving Les in darkness. For Les, the bed and pillows felt like they were made out of the softest marshmallow imaginable, while in his mind, rockets and shooting stars exploded into cascades of beautiful flowers and waterfalls turned into tumbling kaleidoscopes of wonderfully hued hexagrams and pentangles. Shit. How good's this, smiled Les, as a big rocket exploded sending flowers and sparks and colours he'd never seen or imagined before spiralling and spinning everywhere. Next thing, everything went black.

After spending most of the night virtually comatose, Les felt groggy and acutely unsure of where he was when he woke up the next morning. He knew he was in a bed, it was getting on for nine, and apart from his trainers he'd slept in his clothes. That was about it. He raised himself up on his elbows and had a look around. He was in a modest bedroom with a window above the bed, an old wooden wardrobe against one wall and a dressing table against another. A couple of colourful bird prints hung on the walls and a worn red scatter rug covered the wooden floor. He drew back the curtains and gazed out at a sunny day, shining on lush green fields hemmed by sagging wire fences and surrounded by thickly forested hills that rose gradually to a mountain range in the distance. Les shook his head then rubbed his eyes, sat up and swung his legs over the side of the bed. Shit. Where the fuck am I? he asked himself. His trainers were placed neatly beneath the bed. Les stared at them for a moment then laced them on, opened the bedroom door and stepped outside.

He found himself in the corridor of an old house with high ceilings and polished wooden floors. Opposite were two more bedrooms and on the left was a loungeroom then glass double doors led onto a large verandah. On the right was a bathroom and at the end of the hallway a kitchen, where Les could hear talk-back radio. Les stepped into the bathroom to splash some water on his face.

It had a tiny cabinet above the sink with a small window to the side, and a big round shower nozzle sat behind a green plastic curtain covering a claw foot enamel bath. Les soon recognised the face looking back at him in the mirror and threw several handfuls of cold water on it as he tried to kick-start his mind. He rinsed his mouth then dried his face and walked down to the kitchen.

Like the rest of the house, the kitchen was spacious and belonged in the past. A chipped electric stove sat next to a one-tub sink under a small window, a thick wooden cornice ran around the whitewashed walls and an open door on the left led to a set of stairs running down to a backyard. A modern two-door fridge sat opposite the sink, all the appliances were new and in the middle of the kitchen was a solid old wooden table and chairs. Seated at one end of the table, listening to a small radio and drinking coffee from a plunger was Lonnie Lonreghan, dressed in a pair of black cotton cargoes, a plain black T-shirt and a pair of black Converse gym boots. He looked up as Les entered the room and switched off the radio.

'Hello, Les,' he smiled. 'How are you feeling?'

Les shook his head. 'I don't know, Lonnie. Where exactly am I?'

'My place,' replied Lonnie.

'Your place?'

'Yeah. I drove you here last night.'

Les thought for a moment. 'That's right. You did too. But …?'

Lonnie pushed a mug over in front of a chair. 'Sit down and have a cup of coffee,' he said, filling the mug from the plunger.

'Thanks.' There was milk and sugar on the table. Les tipped some into his mug, gave it a stir and took a sip. 'Hey. That's bloody good coffee, Lonnie,' he said.

'Yeah. I get it flown in from New Guinea.' Lonnie pushed two tablets across the table — a small white one and a pink and grey capsule. 'And while you're at it, take these.'

Les frowned at the pills. 'What are they?'

'Duromine and Sudafed.'

'Duromine and Sudafed. My sinuses aren't too bad this morning. And I don't need to lose any weight.' Les took a sip of coffee. 'Hey wait a minute,' he said. 'Did you give me a couple of pills last night?'

'It's all starting to come back to you,' smiled Lonnie.

'Yeah. Sort of,' Les replied cautiously.

'So take the pills, Les. There's a little bit of mild

speed in them. And they'll clear your head after last night.'

Les stared at the two pills. 'Ahh, fuckin why not,' he said. 'I've got a long drive in front of me and I don't know which way's up.' Les picked up the two pills and washed them down with a mouthful of coffee. 'All right, Lonnie,' he said seriously. 'Last night. Exactly what happened?'

'What happened? You stole poor little Amy's choc chip cookies from the snack bar and pigged out on Nimbin biscuits, you goose. That's what happened.'

Lonnie filled Les in on the previous night's events. Including the licensing police arriving, the punters dancing their heads off, Buddy and Mason getting hurt and how Les inadvertently ate all Amy's biscuits.

'I couldn't let you go back to the hotel on your own in your condition,' said Lonnie. 'Those blokes waiting for you would have flogged the shit out of you. And there's no way you could have driven your car. So I bombed you out on Mogadons, brought you back here, and put you to bed before you flipped out and spent the night howling at the moon.'

Les thought for a moment then raised his mug. 'Thanks, Lonnie,' he said. 'Things are starting to fall into place now and that was very good of you. I appreciate it.'

'Don't mention it,' smiled Lonnie.

'And you'll take me back into town shortly?' said Les. 'So I can pick up my stuff. And get the fuck out of beautiful downtown Nimbin.'

'I will, Les,' Lonnie nodded sincerely over his coffee. 'But not for a little while yet.'

'Oh. And why's that, Lonnie?' asked Les.

Lonnie glanced at his watch. 'Because ... in about another hour or so, nine hillbillies will be coming up the front driveway in two cars to murder me.'

'Murder you?' Les was incredulous. 'What the fuck are you talking about?'

'That's why Eddie was supposed to be here last night,' said Lonnie. 'To give me a hand to sort these dills out. Which is why I had the shits when you walked into the office.'

'Oh great,' said Les. 'Now I'm stuck here.'

Lonnie shook his head. 'You're not stuck here, Les. You can leave any time you want. But I need my car. And it's a long walk back to Nimbin.'

Les stared bitterly at Lonnie. 'I don't fuckin believe it.'

Lonnie topped Norton's mug up. 'Bring your coffee out onto the verandah and I'll explain a few things to you.'

'Yeah, all right,' scowled Les.

Les added a little milk to his coffee then followed Lonnie out to the front verandah. There was a pinewood table and chairs in the middle and it commanded a beautiful view over the surrounding hills and valleys. Lonnie leaned against the railing with his coffee and Les joined him.

'You see, Les,' began Lonnie. 'I don't own this house. I've got it on a ten-year lease.'

'A ten-year lease?' said Les.

'Yeah,' replied Lonnie. 'I was in hospital getting a hernia cut out. And the old bloke I was sharing the room with, Hugh, was a digger who'd fought in Korea. And we got to be mates. He's the owner and he was getting a new knee before he went into a nursing home. Anyway, while he was full of morphine and that, he started rambling on about this farm he owned near Nimbin. And how he'd have to let it go because he couldn't handle the stairs and the hills and it was too far away for him to be living on his own. He didn't want to sell it. But he had to.'

'He wasn't married?' asked Les.

Lonnie shook his head. 'His wife died five years ago. And he'd fallen out with his family. Anyway. To make a long story short.' Lonnie tapped the side of his head. 'Hugh was a bit radio ga-ga. So I talked him into leasing the place to me, option to buy.'

'How much is the rent?' asked Les.

'Three twenty a month,' said Lonnie. 'Which gets sent to Hugh at the nursing home in Southport.'

'Fair enough,' agreed Les. 'But why would you want to lease an old joint like this out in the middle of nowhere? You got a bar in town. Couldn't you get a granny flat or something built onto it?'

Lonnie pointed around the side of the house. 'You see that mountain at the back?'

Les looked where Lonnie was pointing. Back behind the house was a steep mountain range and between the trees leading up to it, Les could make out a wide, overgrown track with a rusting rail line running along the middle, missing a number of sleepers.

'Yeah, I see it,' nodded Les. 'What's with the old railway line?'

'Those tracks lead to an old tin mine on the left. And a gold mine on the right.'

'A gold mine?'

'That's right,' nodded Lonnie. 'The old bloke said the tin and gold ran out years ago. But my brother Sam in Brisbane is a geologist. We snuck up here and had a look. The tin's gone. But there's a reef in the old mine they missed with at least ten million dollars' worth of gold in it.'

'Ten million dollars,' said Les. 'Holy shit!'

'Poor old Hugh's none the wiser,' shrugged Lonnie. 'So me and Sam are going to get it out.'

Les sipped his coffee and stared at Lonnie for a moment. 'Lonnie,' he said, easily, 'I'm going to go out on a limb here, but has that shithole of a bar you're running got anything to do with the gold mine?'

Lonnie nodded slowly. 'Very perceptive, Les,' he acknowledged. 'I send all the gold to India through various contacts on the airlines. Then wash the money through the bar. As far as the Taxation Department will know, that shithole of a bar's going to be turning over more money than Jupiter's Casino. By the time they smell a rat, the Double L Ranch will get hit by Jewish lightning. Then it'll be goodbye Nimbin, hello Whitsunday Passage. And please remove your shoes when you board my yacht.'

'In other words, you're going to wash ten million bucks through the bar, burn it down, and spend the rest of your life sailing round the Barrier Reef.'

'My brother's got to get his whack first,' said Lonnie.

Les shook his head. 'Well I'll be buggered.'

'The only thing stopping me is these fuckin clowns lobbing here this morning wanting to kill me.'

'So who are these dills?' asked Les. 'Where are they from? And how do they know what's going on?'

'They're from Stanthorpe,' replied Lonnie.

'I know where that is,' said Les. 'I grew up in Dirranbandi.'

'There's the old bloke's three sons. Three cousins. And three mates. The sons always knew about the old abandoned gold mine. Now they've put two and two together. And figured a city slicker who shared a room in hospital with their old man hasn't taken out a ten-year lease on his rundown farm and opened up a bar in broke-arse Nimbin for the country air. They know what's going on.'

'Yeah. It sure looks that way,' agreed Les.

'So if I disappear, the lease is dissolved, their father's in a home, and they automatically take over the farm. Along with the gold mine.'

'And how do you know they'll be arriving here this morning?'

'My brother Sam's got a mate in Stanthorpe who's had dealings with these arseholes. He knows every move they make.'

'Right,' nodded Les.

'The rotten fuckin thing is, Les,' said Lonnie, 'me and Eddie would have had these cunts on toast.'

'You would?'

A smile flickered in Lonnie's eyes. 'Have you ever read a book, Les, called *The Art of War* by Sun Tzu?'

Les shook his head. 'No. Can't say I have, Lonnie.'

'He was a Chinese philosopher. And two thousand years ago, he wrote a brilliant text for victory on the battlefield, which was translated into English by several different writers.'

'And?'

'He said, if you know the enemy and know yourself, you need not fear the result of a hundred battles. He also said, all warfare is based on deception.'

Suddenly Les felt all his wooziness had disappeared along with any desire to eat. He felt energised, wanting to talk and interested in what Lonnie had to say.

'Go on, Lonnie,' smiled Les. 'Keep talking. This is getting good.'

'Okay,' said Lonnie. 'Well, I know my enemy. And they're nothing but a bunch of inbred fuckin yobbos. And I know myself. I was a damn good soldier. So was Eddie.'

'Nothing wrong with Eddie,' enthused Les. 'Got balls of steel. Go anywhere. Do anything. I've been there with him at times.'

'I know,' said Lonnie. 'And as for deception, I'm telling you, Les, I've got these pricks deceived like you wouldn't believe. They won't know what hit them.'

Les fidgeted around alongside the railing and emphasised his words with short quick hand gestures. 'Lonnie,' he said. 'I'm going to go out on a limb here again. But when you brought me home last night, would the thought possibly have been at the back of your mind of substituting me for Eddie? Seeing as our mutual friend stuffed up his ankle and couldn't make it.'

'Yes,' answered Lonnie.

'I thought so,' Norton smiled thinly.

'But like I said, Les, you don't have to stay. You can leave any time you want. Or go hide up in the bush somewhere till it's all over. Then hitchhike back to Nimbin. However ...'

'However,' cut in Les. 'There's always a fuckin however. What's the however this time — mate?'

'If you stay and help me,' said Lonnie, 'I'll give you quarter of a million dollars.'

'Quarter of a million dollars?' Norton's eyes lit up. 'Shit! That's a lot of chops, Lonnie.'

'That's what I was going to give Eddie. Not right now. When I start getting the gold out and the money washed. But that shouldn't be more than a few months down the track.'

'A quarter of a million dollars in just a few months' time,' Les said quietly. 'I could look at that as a kind of … holiday pay.'

'Except this holiday pay is tax free — mate.'

'A quarter of a million dollars, tax free.' Les stared at Lonnie and had a quick think. Very quick. 'All right, Lonnie,' he replied. 'You got me. What's the plan?'

Lonnie grinned and took Norton's hand. 'Good on you, Les,' he said, pumping it vigorously. 'I was hoping you'd come round.' Lonnie rubbed his hands together with glee. 'Okay,' he smiled. 'Here's the first part of the deception. These dills don't know the bar closes at twelve. They think it's open till three and I'll get home after four half-pissed and get to bed about five. Then when they get here, I'll still be in bed snoring my head off. But no. Uncle Lonnie will be up and about organising his welcoming committee.'

'Aha!' exclaimed Les.

'Now. The second part of the deception.' Lonnie pointed towards the driveway coming in. 'You see the gate about half a click down there, amongst the trees?'

Les could just make it out beneath all the branches. 'Yeah. Hey. I remember now. You got out of the car last night and opened it.'

'That's right. Now you see the old Kingswood behind the Colorado?'

'Yeah.'

'I'm going to park it nose-first in front of the gate, unlocked and with the keys in the ignition. But with a flat battery. When they stop to open the gate and one of them goes to move the car and finds it won't start, the rest will get out to push it. That's when we'll jump them. And get them in a crossfire.'

'A crossfire?' said Les.

'Yes.' Lonnie pointed to the gate again. 'You see how the ground slopes up on the right into steep hills. And on the left it levels out towards the main road.'

'I do,' nodded Les.

'Well, I'll be up on the hillside firing down. You'll be on the level ground firing across. That way we get them in a crossfire without any risk of shooting each other.'

'Is that one of Sun Tzu's philosophies?' asked Les.

Lonnie shook his head. 'No. Even though he wrote the six rules of terrain. And preceding your adversary. It's just the natural thing to do under the circumstances.'

'Cool.'

'Then when our little shindig's over, we put the bodies in their cars. I've rigged the old tin mine with explosives. We drive the cars into the mine. I press the button. And boom. Out of sight. Out of mind. Nobody will find them in a hundred years.'

'Sounds good,' said Les. 'But they're going to be armed up. And it won't take all nine of them to push a car out the road. Some are going to be standing round with guns.'

'Of course,' agreed Lonnie. 'Bolt action rifles. They won't take a chance of driving here in two cars full of automatic weapons. If they happen to get pulled over, they'll just want to look like a bunch of fun-loving weekend sports shooters, out to kill something.'

'Fair enough,' agreed Les. 'But guns are guns. They can still put horrible big holes in you.'

'Which is where the next part of the deception arises,' grinned Lonnie. 'Come back to the kitchen, Les. I got something to show you.'

'Righto,' said Les, emptying the last of his coffee over the railing.

Norton followed Lonnie to the kitchen and sat down while Lonnie went to the spare room. The bar owner returned a few minutes later carrying a bulky ammunition case with Russian writing on the side and a smaller one with Chinese writing on it. He placed the cases side by side on the table and opened the bigger one. Packed into the black foam rubber lining were two submachine guns, a pair of silencers and four drum magazines. Lonnie took one of the machine guns out, clicked a drum magazine into the feed lip, checked the safety and handed it to Les.

'What do you think of that, Les?' beamed Lonnie, taking a seat at the table.

Les cradled the submachine gun in his arms and examined it. It had a stove pipe barrel with a thread at the end, a wooden stock, not much in the way of sights and a long trigger guard behind the drum magazine. There were no scratches on the metal or nicks in the stock and it looked brand new.

'I've seen these before,' said Les. 'It's a burp gun. The Chinese used them during the Korean war.'

'The old PPSh–41,' smiled Lonnie. 'Designed by Georgiy Shpagin. Blowback action and a hinged receiver for easy maintenance. Very good, Les. But have you noticed anything just a little different?'

Les moved the gun around and sighted the window above the sink. 'It's very light. And it seems ... kind of small somehow.'

238

'Right on, grasshopper,' smiled Lonnie. 'The original PPSh–41 fires 7.62mm ammo at 900 rpm. Effective range 120m. This little sucker fires plain old garden variety .22 ammo at 180 rpm. Effective range 75m. But,' said Lonnie, poking a finger in the air for emphasis, 'I got five thousand rounds of teflon-tipped bullets. Stop you dead in your tracks, pussycat.'

Les handed the weapon back to Lonnie. 'So where did you get the fuckin things? I know a little bit about guns. But I've never seen anything like this.'

'I got them and the bullets made in Pakistan. At a town called Quetta. Just across the Afghanistan border from Kandahar.'

'They cost much?'

Lonnie shook his head. 'Not really. I had the blueprints for the old PPSh–41. And I just got the gunmaker to knock me up four versions to fire .22s. Along with a few bullets.'

'How did you get them into Australia?' asked Les.

'Contacts,' winked Lonnie. He removed a silencer from the ammunition box and stood up. 'Come on out the backyard, I'll show you something.'

'Okay.' Les rose from the table and excitedly followed Lonnie down the stairs at the rear of the kitchen.

The fence Les had noticed from the bedroom window ran around the back of the house. There was an old shed on the right and on the left an abandoned chicken coop that still stank of chicken shit. A large galvanised-iron water tank sat on the right of the stairs and beyond the house picturesque mountains and valleys rose and fell into the distance. Scattered around the backyard were a number of watermelons and running alongside the fence were about the same number of big blue pumpkins. Lonnie handed Les the submachine gun while he plucked three fat pumpkins from their vines and sat them on top of the fence posts near the old shed.

'Hey, this is nice out here,' said Les, bending down and touching his toes with the submachine gun. 'I'd love to go for a run around those hills and valleys early in the morning when it's cool. It'd be fantastic. You'd take off.'

'How are your sinuses?' asked Lonnie.

Les sucked a huge, healthy lungful of air in through his nose. 'Pretty good to tell you the truth. In fact I feel pretty good all round. Those little pills are working a treat.'

'Excellent,' smiled Lonnie. He took the machine gun from Les, screwed the suppressor onto the barrel, cocked the weapon and slipped the safety. 'Now, Les,' he asked. 'Would you say the skin of a pumpkin is just a little bit tougher than a human being's?'

'Ohh, shit yeah,' answered Les. 'I'd much rather punch some bloke in the head than hit a fuckin pumpkin.'

'Okay. Watch this.' Lonnie raised the machine gun to his shoulder, sighted in the pumpkin on the fence post to the left and gently squeezed the trigger.

The sound was negligible, no more than someone tapping their hand on a table, followed by a constant whack as the bullets slammed into the pumpkin. The .22s weren't heavy enough to send the pumpkin flying. Instead, the teflon-tipped bullets simply tore it to pieces. Les watched fascinated as the shell casings arced up in the air to Lonnie's right and the fat pumpkin was soon whittled down to half its size.

'Holy shit,' said Les, sniffing the cordite when Lonnie stopped firing. 'That bastard of a thing is deadly.'

The smile on Lonnie's face, behind the thin mist of blue smoke rising from the machine gun's barrel, meant business. 'That was a big, heavy pumpkin,' he said. 'Imagine what it would do to your head.'

'Blow it right off your shoulders,' said Les.

'The drum magazine on a PPSh–41 holds seventy-one rounds,' said Lonnie. 'The magazine on this holds a hundred and fifty. At three rounds a second, you can fire this all day. And those sneaky little teflon bullets give you a lot of bang for your buck.'

'Unreal.'

'It's all part of the deception, Les,' smiled Lonnie. 'There'll be a bit of blood and guts flying around. But those dopes wanting to kill me don't know what they're in for. Here.' Lonnie handed the submachine gun to Les. 'Have a shot.'

'Okay.' Les took the weapon and checked the safety. He sighted on the next pumpkin, gripped the magazine and squeezed the trigger.

There was virtually no recoil while before Norton's eyes the pumpkin on the fence post disintegrated. He dropped the machine gun to waist level and blasted the next pumpkin to pieces, putting a few rounds into the fence post while he was at it.

'Not bad, Les,' said Lonnie. 'You've really got the hang of it.'

'You can't miss,' replied Les, pointing the barrel down. 'Plus we've fired off a heap of rounds, and there's petrol left in the tank.'

'A hundred and fifty rounds per magazine,' said Lonnie. He took the weapon from Les. 'All right. Let's go back to the kitchen. I got something else for you.'

'Yo de man, Lonnie,' said Les, trotting up the stairs behind Lonnie. 'Yo de man, baby.'

Back in the kitchen, Lonnie placed the submachine gun on the table while Les poured himself a large glass of water. Lonnie left Les to drink it and went back to the spare room, returning with a pair of long-sleeved green overalls, a pair of old Nike gym boots and a black bandana.

'There you go, mate,' he said, placing everything on the table. 'We can't have you crawling around in the shit and dirt wearing your good clothes.'

'Overalls?' said Les, examining the clothing.

'Yeah. When I was getting the bar built I got one of the chippies to do a bit of work on the house. He left them here along with his gym boots. He was about your size. So they should fit.'

'I'll put them on now.'

Les went to his room and got changed. When he came back, Lonnie had placed the other submachine gun on the table with a silencer attached and a drum magazine in the feed lip. He'd also opened the other case, and sitting on the table were two green ammunition holders resembling a cut-away fisherman's vest with four wide pockets on the front secured by press studs.

'Everything fit all right?' said Lonnie, looking up at Les in his overalls and bandana tied round his head.

Les placed a gym-boot clad foot on one of the chairs. 'Yeah. But what size feet did the cunt have?' he laughed. 'You could put oars on these bloody things and row them.'

'At least you've got a good grip on Australia,' replied Lonnie. 'Okay,' he said, standing up. 'I'll run you through the weapon again and we'll go back over the plan. Then you can zip yourself into your ammo holder, throw some dirt on your face, and you'll be ready to rumble.'

'Sounds good to me, Lonnie,' enthused Les. 'I can't wait.'

Lonnie got Les to change magazines, swapping them with the ones in the ammunition vest. He took Les back out onto the verandah and suggested where Les should lie in hiding at the side of the gate. Lonnie would be up in the hills looking down as planned. He'd give Les a whistle. As soon as he heard it, that's when they'd both open fire. He told Les to keep his head down, move around and try not to shoot up the cars as they had to drive them up to the mine. Then they went back to the kitchen.

'Shit. I wish I had my camera here,' said Les, catching his reflection in the kitchen window. 'I'd love to show this to Eddie.'

'I got one in my room,' said Lonnie. Lonnie went to his room and returned with a digital camera the same as Norton's. 'Get the gun and come back out onto the verandah.'

Norton's face broke into a grin. 'Yeah, baby,' he said, rising from the table. He adjusted his black bandana, picked up his submachine gun and followed Lonnie back out to the verandah.

Lonnie took four photos of Les in various poses with the weapon and let Les take a couple of him. When they'd finished, Lonnie checked his watch and suggested it might be a good idea to run the old Kingswood down to the gate. Les returned the weapon to the kitchen then followed Lonnie down to the front of the house. The station wagon was parked nose-first to the driveway. They gave it a push to get it going and with Lonnie behind the wheel, coasted down to the gate, parking it in the middle of the driveway, between the two thick wooden poles supporting the gate. Leaving the keys in the ignition, Lonnie pulled the handbrake on tight and they got out.

'The gate swings down and to the right,' said Lonnie. 'So when they open it, there'll be plenty of room for them to stand around exposed.' He pointed to the trees and bushes on the level side of the driveway. 'You want to have a quick look around, Les, and familiarise yourself with your firing area?'

'Yeah. Good idea,' agreed Les.

Norton moved around the trees and boulders, noting where different ones were and putting them between himself and the driveway. He checked the tree canopy for light and made sure there were no ant hills around for him to unsuspectingly throw himself on, then rejoined Lonnie, who was making sure the lock and chain on the gate were secure.

'You can bet your life those bastards will have bolt cutters,' he complained. 'Which means I'll have to buy another lock and chain. More bloody expense. Fair dinkum, Les. It never ends.'

'Yes. It's sad, Lonnie,' sympathised Les. 'But with ten million dollars' worth of gold about to fall in, I think you can afford it.'

Lonnie pointed up to the old home. 'Come on,' he winked. 'Let's jog back to the house. Get our blood circulating.'

'Hey. I'll be in that,' said Les.

Despite having his ammunition belt on and a pair of gym boots three sizes too big for him, Les jogged up the driveway with ease and would have liked to have kept going. Lonnie went with him stride for stride and neither of them would have blown out a candle when they reached the parking area in front of the house.

'Hey, you're not in bad shape for an old bloke,' joked Les. 'I'm half full of speed and you were starting to get away from me in the finish.'

'I used to run marathons a while back,' said Lonnie. 'Didn't win many. But I always finished in the top ten.'

'Fair dinkum?' Les pointed to his mouth. 'Mate. I got to have another drink of water. I'm drier than a bunch of artificial flowers.'

'I'm a bit that way myself,' said Lonnie.

They took the stairs up to the house and went straight to the kitchen. Les had one glass of water then poured himself another. Lonnie also poured himself a glass. Les had another drink then glanced at his watch.

'How long before you reckon they'll be here?' he asked.

'Not long,' answered Lonnie. 'Let's go back out onto the verandah.'

'Okay.'

They stood on the verandah, taking in the sun while they drank water and quietly discussed things. Les was about to drill Lonnie over a couple of matters that had been nagging him, when Lonnie stiffened and any expression drained from his face.

'They're here,' he said bluntly.

'They are?' replied Les. 'How do you know?'

Lonnie pointed to where the driveway turned off from the road. 'See that flock of sulphur crested cockatoos down there?'

Les stared out over the valley to where twenty big white parrots were circling noisily above the trees, their raucous screeching echoing all the way up to the house.

'Yeah,' replied Les. 'There's got to be a couple of dozen of them.'

'Well, they're my guard dogs.' Lonnie turned to Norton. 'Okay, Les,' he said seriously. 'It's show time. Let's go.'

Les swallowed the rest of his water. 'Righto.'

They hurried back to the kitchen. Lonnie zipped into his ammunition vest, put his bandana on, then they both picked up their submachine guns and double-timed it out of the house. Next thing Les was running down the driveway behind Lonnie till they stopped at the front gate.

'Okay, Les,' said Lonnie, pointing to the hills on his right. 'I'm going to be up there looking down. As soon as you hear me whistle, pour it into the cunts. And don't worry about wasting ammo. You've got heaps.'

'No worries,' replied Les.

'And don't forget to rub a bit of dirt on your face.'

'Okey doke.'

Les watched Lonnie scramble up the slope then quickly moved back into the bush about fifteen metres from the gate. He found a concealed position between a clump of boulders and a gum tree, cocked his weapon and lay down on his stomach, picking up some dirt as Lonnie had told him and smearing it across his face. After wiping his hands on his overalls, Les readied his weapon again and waited, and although he felt upbeat and ready to go, the gravity of what he was about to do suddenly sank in. This wasn't a game of paintball. This was the real thing. And quarter of a million dollars or not, he was about to help a bloke he'd only just met murder nine men in cold blood. It might have been some twisted form of self-defence. But it was still murder and if the law ever caught up with Lonnie, they could both finish up in gaol. Besides that, if things went wrong, he could cop a bullet in the head himself or get his stomach blown apart. Fair dinkum, sweated Les. Can I get myself into some situations. And all over a lousy fuckin frog. You can't tell me that's not karma. Les brushed away a fly as two kookaburras started a heated argument in a nearby tree. Suddenly the kookaburras stopped arguing when two cars appeared moving slowly up the driveway.

Neither vehicle was late model. The first was a dark blue Ford station wagon with decals all over it. The following car was a black Ford sedan with a luggage rack on top. The station wagon stopped a little before the gate and the driver cut the motor. The second car pulled up behind and its driver did the same.

His adrenalin now squirting around in the pit of his stomach, Les watched intensely as a tall skinny man wearing a brown baseball cap and blue bib-and-brace overalls over a matching T-shirt, got out from behind the wheel of the station wagon. Another, shorter man in a dark T-shirt and black jeans got out of the passenger side carrying a pair of bolt cutters, leaving three men seated in the back.

Another man in jeans and a blue flannelette shirt got out from behind the wheel of the sedan, leaving another man seated in the front and three in the back.

Peering through the scrub Les was able to count ten men instead of nine and imagined Lonnie would have no trouble doing the same. The first three men went into a quiet huddle. From his position between the rocks and the gum tree, Les couldn't quite hear what they were saying. But he watched the man with the bolt cutters snip the lock and chain, as Lonnie had predicted, and kick it to one side of the driveway before he swung the gate back. The man in overalls walked across to the Kingswood and peered in the driver's side window, then opened the door and got behind the wheel. A second or two later, Les heard the slow dull whine of a starter motor trying to kick over. The man in overalls soon gave up then got out of the Kingswood and walked back to the two men at the gate. Les still couldn't quite pick up their voices, but he had a pretty good idea what they were saying, because the man in overalls went to the station wagon and the man in the flannelette shirt walked back to the sedan. Next thing, the remaining seven men got out of the two cars carrying weapons, some of which they handed to the first three men, then as Lonnie had predicted again, all ten men gathered in front of the open gate. Les studied them intently.

They were all dressed in the same dark clothing and each had the same slow dull-witted look about him. Les put their ages at around thirty, except for two carrying pump-action shotguns. One had long straggly blond hair, the other's hair was cropped into a brown mullet and both wouldn't have been more than eighteen; the man with the brown mullet had a distinctive face full of acne and would be lucky if he was that old.

Beads of sweat trickled down Norton's face attracting more flies and Les would have given anything to swat the annoying little insects as he forced himself to remain motionless. The seconds began to feel like hours while the men formed perfect targets standing around the open gate and Les began to worry Lonnie might have got distracted by something. Come on, Lonnie, Les urged silently. We won't get a better opportunity than this. Les moved the barrel of his submachine gun a fraction, figuring to take out the man wearing overalls first, then work the weapon left. Despite the bandana, more sweat trickled down Norton's face and a fly landed next to his eye. Les blinked hard several times to dislodge it and his concern for Lonnie rose as the men appeared not to bother about moving the old Kingswood. Then Norton heard Lonnie's short sharp whistle echo down the hillside. The men reacted and turned to each other as Norton let go a sigh of relief. That'll do me, smiled Les. He lined up the man in overalls and squeezed the trigger for two seconds.

Six teflon-tipped bullets slammed into the man's chest almost ripping his heart and lungs out. He gave a quick scream, dropped his rifle then collapsed straight onto his behind and fell backwards, dead. Les moved the silenced submachine gun to the left and stitched the next man across the chest, who fell down in a fast spreading pool of blood on top of the man in overalls. With bullets clanging into the gate and kicking up dirt around their feet, other men started screaming and falling as Les and Lonnie poured a steady stream of bullets into them. Panic-stricken, the remaining men began firing blindly into the hills and bushes on either side of the driveway and around the gate as they dived for cover.

Les shot another man's face off and wounded another in the legs when he ran towards the Ford sedan behind the young bloke with the acned face. The wounded man fell down against the sedan and, through his pain, started firing in Norton's direction. Two bullets ricocheted off the boulders on Norton's left, and another buried itself in the gum tree. Les quickly figured the only way the wounded man would have spotted him was the arc of shells flying up in the air then landing in the surrounding bush. Les rolled away to his left, just as a blast of shotgun pellets tore apart the bush where he'd been lying, followed by another which blew away a small tree. Les raised the submachine gun and stitched the man he'd wounded from his groin up to his chin, slicing him open like a watermelon, then Les rolled to the right as another two blasts from the shotgun ripped into the surrounding bush. Les went to fire a burst in the direction of the shotgun's noise and found he'd emptied the magazine. Swiftly he changed magazines then rolled away once more as another two blasts from the shotgun ripped into the bush and scorched slivers of granite into grainy clouds of dust from the boulders where he'd been lying. On the other side of the driveway, Les could hear men screaming in pain, guns going off and teflon-tipped bullets thumping into the ground and slamming into the station wagon. He surmised Lonnie had everything under control, so he concentrated on the kid with the shotgun, intent on nailing him before he took off down the driveway and brought everything undone. Cradling his weapon, Les sprinted in a half crouch through the bush till he was a few metres past the black Ford and flopped down behind another gum tree. Suddenly everything went quiet.

'Hey, Les,' Lonnie called out, from up on the hillside. 'You all right?'

'Yeah. Good as gold,' Les yelled back. 'How's yourself?'

'I'm all right. I think they're all dead over this side. What about you?'

'I've got one with a shotgun near the black Ford. Watch out for him. And watch out for me.'

'Roger that.'

Roger that, mused Les. Where does Lonnie think he is? Viet-fuckin-nam? Now, where's this pimply-faced little shit with the shotgun? Two blasts from the shotgun sailed over Norton's head into the trees telling Les someone was firing from down too low. He snuck his head around the tree and stared at the black Ford. A moving shadow beneath it told Les all he needed to know. He aimed the submachine gun and fired a long burst beneath the car's chassis. A haphazard blast from the shotgun, followed by a shout of pain, told Les he'd struck pay dirt.

'Hey, Lonnie,' Les yelled out. 'I think I got him. I'm coming towards the back of the old Ford. Okay?'

'I'm on you,' Lonnie's voice called back.

Slowly Les stood up and with finger on the trigger, advanced slowly and carefully towards the rear of the black Ford. When he got to the car he saw a denim-covered leg and a shotgun barrel sticking out from under the left rear door, just as Lonnie appeared, stepping around the bodies on his side of the driveway.

'Shit,' said Lonnie. 'What a mess.'

'You can say that again,' agreed Les. He pointed his gun at the leg poking out from beneath the black Ford. 'There were ten shooters and that's the last of them. The kid with the shotgun.'

'Yeah. Let's take a look at him.' Lonnie kicked the barrel of the shotgun to one side then took hold of the kid's leg by his jeans and yanked him out from under the car. One hand was almost shot off, he'd taken two bullets in his left leg and one through his ribs, but he was still breathing. 'Well, I'll be buggered,' said Lonnie. 'Look at that. He's still alive.'

'Unbelievable.' Les shook his head and stared down at the unfortunate young bloke lying bleeding on the driveway.

'Ohh, give me a break will you, mister,' begged the young bloke. 'Please. I'm hurting something awful.'

'Sure,' replied Lonnie. 'We'll stop the bleeding and get you to a hospital in no time.'

'Thanks, mister,' sniffed the young bloke. 'I didn't want to be here in the first place. They forced me.'

'They forced you?' said Les.

'Yeah. I'm only seventeen.'

'Shit. That's a bit young to be running around firing shotguns at people,' chastised Les.

'I know,' sniffed the young bloke.

'Have you got any HCF?' Lonnie asked him.

'What?'

'Have you got any HCF? Are you in Medibank Private?' asked Lonnie.

The young bloke shook his head. 'No, I ain't, mister,' he coughed.

'Well, you should be.' Lonnie brought his submachine gun up and put six rounds in the young bloke's heart, killing him instantly.

Les looked at what was left of the young bloke's chest beneath the holes in his black T-shirt, slowly shook his head and turned to Lonnie. 'Do you think he feels better now?'

'I'm not sure,' replied Lonnie. 'I certainly hope so.' Lonnie clicked his still smoking weapon onto semi-auto then walked around the bodies and pumped a couple of bullets into the heads of any he thought still showed signs of life. Satisfied they were all dead, he returned to Les.

'Everything sweet?' Les asked.

'Yes. Everyone is resting comfortably,' answered Lonnie.

'You know, it's funny,' said Les, taking in the carnage around him. 'When I first moved to Sydney I had this phobia about dead bodies. But after knocking around with Eddie, I started getting used to them.'

'That's understandable,' conceded Lonnie. 'Okay, Les,' he said. 'If you'll start throwing the bodies in their cars, along with all their guns, I'll back the Kingswood up to the house and get it out the road, then come back and give you a hand. Then we'll drive both cars into the old tin mine and — ka-boom.'

'Okay,' replied Les.

'And the sooner we get this done,' smiled Lonnie, 'the sooner we can sit back and have a nice cup of coffee, or whatever.'

'Sounds good to me,' said Les.

Lonnie took Norton's weapon and ammunition vest, placed them in the Kingswood with his, then got behind the wheel and rolled it forward in front of the station wagon. He got out, opened the back of the Kingswood and took out two pairs of gardening gloves and a set of jumper leads. He tossed one pair of gloves to Les, popped both bonnets and in no time had the leads connected and the Kingswood's motor started. He disconnected the leads, got behind the wheel of the Kingswood and started reversing the old car back up the driveway to the house, leaving Les with the grisly chore of loading the bodies and body parts into the two cars.

The teflon bullets had done their work well and Norton's task wasn't enjoyable in the least. Some bodies had limbs almost severed or hands blown off. Others had bony lumps of red meat sitting on their shoulders where their heads had been and others were oozing blood and entrails from beneath their torn clothing. Les recognised one bloke he'd shot in the face by his Bon Jovi T-shirt, and what the teflon-tipped bullets had left of his teeth and jaw bone made the bloke look like something from a movie about the undead. Working fast, Les piled everything into the back of the two cars leaving only the body of the unfortunate young bloke Lonnie finished off. Les was about to toss him in the front of the black Ford when Lonnie walked through the gate.

'Hey. Looks like you've finished already,' he said. 'You don't muck around, mate.'

'No. It's not something you'd take your time over.' Les pointed to the young bloke lying next to the sedan. 'There's one left. You want to give me a hand to toss him in the front?'

'Fuck putting him in the front and have him flop all over you when you're driving.' Lonnie nodded to the roof of the car. 'He's not very big. Throw him up on the luggage rack?'

'Good idea.' Les took the young bloke's arms, Lonnie took his legs, then they swung him back before landing him face down in the luggage rack. 'Okay,' said Les. 'What now?'

'I'll get in the station wagon. You take the other heap and follow me up the driveway and round the back of the house into the tin mine. It goes back about half a click.'

'Righto.' Les checked himself out. He was smeared with blood from head to foot. 'Shit. I'm glad you had those overalls and gloves. Have a look at me. You'd think I just slaughtered a goat.'

'Yes. You're a mess all right,' agreed Lonnie. 'But I got to tell you something, Les. I was watching you from up on the hill. You were fuckin unreal. Rolling and shooting at the same time. Unbelievable.' He reached across and shook Norton's hand. 'You sure you weren't ever in the armed forces?'

'Yeah,' nodded Les. 'B Battalion. Be here when they go. Be here when they get back.'

'Come on,' chuckled Lonnie. 'Let's get this shit out the road. Then we can get cleaned up.'

'Let's,' nodded Les.

Lonnie got into the station wagon and Les climbed behind the wheel of the sedan. The keys were in the ignition and the old car started instantly then purred like a kitten. Les gave it a couple of revs before he slipped it into drive and started following Lonnie up the driveway. Shit, this isn't a bad old bus, thought Les, checking out the stereo and the interior. Goes all right. Got a good luggage rack on the roof too. Seems a pity to bury it. They reached the house then Lonnie went left around it, before entering the old track between the trees Les had seen earlier.

Les followed Lonnie along the track and they started bumping over the old rail lines which caused the wet bodies in the back of the car to start sliding around all over the place. The young bloke in the luggage rack moved forward and a bloodied hand appeared on top of the windscreen. After about five hundred metres the rail lines came out at a wide clearing in front of the mountain behind the house, scattered with corroded oil drums, sheets of rusty metal, wire, sleepers and other detritus you would expect to find around two old mines. The shaft leading into the tin mine on the left was about the same size as a double garage, the shaft into the gold mine was smaller with no rail lines. Les followed Lonnie into the tin mine and after a few metres of bumping over wooden beams, Lonnie switched on his headlights. So did Les. A few hundred metres further, the shaft ended at a wall of solid rock. Lonnie pulled up, cut the engine and got out of the station wagon, leaving the headlights on, and Les did the same. Lonnie closed the door and clicked on a torch and the light picked up tiny flecks of colour along the sides of the shaft. Standing in the cool silence, Les could hear the euphonious plop of water dripping from the ceiling into puddles amongst the old rail lines.

'No need for the torch, Lonnie,' said Les, pointing behind him. 'I can see light at the end of the tunnel.'

'So can I,' replied Lonnie. 'But I want to check these out.' Lonnie shone the torch on a sausage-shaped length of greasy brown paper with a diode jammed in it, attached to one of the beams.

'What is it?' asked Les. 'Semtex? Or some other exotic explosive you've had smuggled in from the subcontinent?'

'No. Just plain old garden variety dynamite,' replied Lonnie. 'Actually, I found it under the house. My brother got me the semiconductors.'

'That was handy,' commented Les.

'Yeah.' With Les following, Lonnie started walking towards the entrance, stopping to shine the torch on all the dynamite he'd attached to different beams. 'Well. Everything looks A-okay,' he finally said. 'Let's go outside and watch the fireworks.'

'Righty oh.'

They walked outside into the sunlight and Les followed Lonnie over to the trail. They got behind a tree and Lonnie took a remote the same size as a mini-cassette from the side pocket of his cargoes. He pulled out a short aerial, flicked a switch and a red light came on.

'Okay, Les,' he smiled. 'On my mark. Three-two-one.'

Lonnie pushed a black button and an explosion rumbled through the mine shaft, the mountain shook and a great cloud of dust and debris came flying out of the entrance to the mine shaft spreading dust and rocks all around the clearing.

Rocks pinged into some of the rusty oil drums and more debris flew past the tree where Les and Lonnie were sheltered.

'Beautiful,' beamed Lonnie. 'Couldn't be ...'

He'd no sooner spoken than another explosion rocked the mine shaft. The mountain above shuddered, several boulders came tumbling down into the clearing along with a few dead branches and more dust came swirling out of the mine shaft. On the right, another cloud of dust rolled slowly out of the entrance to the gold mine.

'Great green gravy, Batman,' said Les. 'How much bloody dynamite did you use?'

Still gripping the remote, Lonnie stared wide-eyed at Les. 'That fuckin well wasn't me,' he cursed. 'It was them. The dirty low cunts. They had the same fuckin idea.'

'What? Bury you in the mine shaft?' said Les.

'Yeah. The bastards. I didn't even think to check the boot of that old bomb Ford. It was full of explosives.' Lonnie stared across at the dust still rising from the entrance to the second shaft. 'Oh no,' he wailed. 'Not the fuckin gold mine.'

Lonnie pocketed the remote and sprinted over to the second shaft. Les followed him across the clearing while Lonnie ran inside the entrance. He returned a minute or two later, long-faced and covered in dust.

'Trouble?' Les asked quietly.

'Yes,' Lonnie nodded bleakly. 'You could say that.'

'You can't get the gold?'

'Oh no. I can still get the gold out. But it's going to take a lot longer than I anticipated. And I'm going to have to hire a team of fuckin morons to dig through the rubble.'

'Oh bugger.'

'Yeah,' replied Lonnie. 'Bugger.'

'So my quarter of a million dollars in holiday pay,' suggested Les, 'has now turned into — more of a superannuation fund?'

'I'm afraid so, Les,' admitted Lonnie. 'I'm afraid fuckin so.'

Despite everything turning pear shaped Les couldn't help a chuckle. 'Don't worry, Lonnie. I knew it was too good to be true. I just knew it.'

'Sorry, Les. But you will get your dough.'

'I know.' Les placed his arm around Lonnie's shoulder. 'Come on, mate,' he said. 'Put it behind you for the time being. Let's go and get cleaned up. And have a cuppa.'

'Yeah, why not,' muttered Lonnie. He drew away from Les, stood in the clearing with his fists clenched by his side and railed up at the sky. 'Why do you hate me so much?' he howled. 'Why?'

'While you're there, Lonnie,' said Les. 'Mention my name as well.'

They walked back to the house. Les climbed out of his blood-soaked clothes and gave them to Lonnie to burn. Les had a welcome shower, then got changed into his jeans and denim shirt and joined Lonnie in the kitchen where the bar owner had made a fresh plunger of coffee. Les sat down, poured himself a mug, added milk and sugar and stared across the table at Lonnie.

'Well, Lonnie,' said Les, taking a sip. 'What can I say? All's well that ends well. At least you got rid of those idiots. And we're still alive.'

'Yeah. I guess that's one way of looking at it.' The hint of a smile flickered across Lonnie's face. 'You know, Les,' he said. 'I got a bottle of Jack Daniel's single barrel there. And some good dope. I don't smoke it much. But it's almost noon. Why don't we get a bit high?'

'Sort of — high noon in Nimbin?' replied Les.

'Yeah,' replied Lonnie. 'That's one way of looking at it.' The bar owner reached behind him and took a small tin container from a drawer. He placed it on the table and took out two spliffs and a Bic lighter. 'There you are, Les,' he said. 'Help yourself.'

Les stared at the two joints and disdainfully shook his head. 'No thanks,' he replied. 'I've had enough dope and shit to last me for the next ten years. In fact, if you don't mind, Lonnie, I'd like to fuck off.'

Lonnie looked at the joints for a second, then put them back in the container. 'Yeah, fair enough. Hey look, Les,' he said. 'I'm really sorry about what happened. But like I told you. You will get your money. I promise.'

'Hey, Lonnie,' smiled Les. 'I trust you. You're not the best bloke I ever met. But I do trust you.'

'Thanks, Les. That's very nice of you.'

Les stared at Lonnie over the top of his mug. 'But while I've got you here, there's a couple of things I'd like to know.'

'Sure, Les,' Lonnie shrugged. 'What's that?'

'Why would you want to bring me all this way to spend two nights recording music? It doesn't make sense. You could get a monkey out of Taronga Park to do what I just did.'

'Yes. And if I'd have got someone from round here to do it that's exactly what I would have got. A monkey out of a zoo. I just wanted eight hours of good rock 'n roll music I can play at the bar. And play for myself at home. And I didn't want it fucked up.'

'Be pretty hard to fuck it up,' said Les.

'Maybe,' shrugged Lonnie. 'But I also wanted someone I could rely on if Mason and Buddy got into any trouble. I know how good you are. And Eddie said you owed him a favour. So here you are, mate.'

'Yes,' nodded Les. 'Reliability is one of my worst faults.'

'And if you're wondering why I got you to book into the hotel instead of letting you stay here, me and Eddie didn't want you to get involved. Only two people were supposed to know about this little action. Me and Eddie. If you'd have been staying here, like last night for instance, you could have got caught up in everything.'

'I did anyway,' said Les.

'Yeah. But you know what I mean,' countered Lonnie.

'Fair enough. But the other thing. The one that's really burning my arse. Why play all that rockin get-down music and not let anyone dance to it? You even put signs up. I mean, that's plain fuckin crazy.'

Lonnie tossed back his head and laughed. 'I did that for the licensing cops.'

'For the licensing police?' queried Les. 'What do you mean?'

'Remember the two cops that came in last night?'

'Yeah.'

'Well, the one in the grey suit, Detective Landstra, thanks to all the dope in Nimbin, he gave me all this grief because he was convinced I was starting up a disco where I could move ecstasy and pills to ravers. He wasn't worried the place was a shithouse. But he jumped up and down and said if he caught anyone in there with so much as an aspirin, if he even caught one raver dancing in the joint, he'd be all over me like flies on shit.

'I said fair enough. I won't let anyone dance in the place. I won't even let them clap their hands, tap their feet or click their fingers.

'He told me not to be a fuckin smartarse and just keep my nose clean. Or else.'

'Or else,' echoed Les.

'Yeah. So I put those signs up and stopped people from dancing. And when Landstra and his mate gave me a visit on Saturday night, to prove I was his faithful servant and intended obeying his every word to the very letter of the law, I showed him the No Dancing signs as instructed. Now he doesn't know whether I'm a complete idiot. Or a good bloke. But it worked,' smiled Lonnie. 'Because from here on he'll leave me alone. And the punters can smoke pot and dance on the ceiling for all I give a fuck.'

'Unbelievable,' said Les. 'I learn something new every day.'

'You sure do, mate.'

Les took a sip of coffee. 'While I was in the shower, something else did occur to me.'

'What was that?' asked Lonnie.

'What happens when those ten blokes are reported missing?'

'I don't know,' shrugged Lonnie. 'What will happen? My brother found out what they had planned. But I doubt if they would have advertised the fact they were coming round here to kill me. And if I do get a visit from the wallopers — which wouldn't be for weeks or months anyway — I won't know what they're talking about. And what are they going to find? They're not going to dig up the old tin mine. They'd need a corps of engineers to do that. And they're not going to go to all that trouble for those dills anyway. They'll probably be glad to see the arse end of them. Taken by a UFO. I'll go down and pick up all those shell casings. And by then the rain will have washed all the blood away. Those pricks from Stanthorpe would have been in more trouble explaining what happened when I went missing.'

'Yeah. I guess you're right,' agreed Les.

'So like you say, Les, all's well that ends well.' Lonnie put his mug of coffee down and rose from the table. 'Wait here a minute. I got something for you.' Lonnie rose from the table and returned with an envelope and a small leather bag which he placed on the table in front of Les. 'There you go, mate. Your thousand dollars. And a small bonus.'

Les gave the money a cursory glance then opened the leather pouch and removed the contents. 'Hey. Gold nuggets,' he said, watching them gleam in the sunlight coming through the kitchen window. 'Fuckin unreal.'

'There's a couple of ounces there. Which proves the gold's in the mine and you just gotta hang in for a while.' Lonnie took a sip of coffee. 'So are we square for the time being, mate?'

Les nudged the gold nuggets with his finger and looked directly at Lonnie. 'No. Not really,' he said.

'Oh?' Lonnie was a little surprised.

'There is one more thing you could do for me.'

'Sure, Les. What's that?'

'Can you burn me a copy of all that grouse music I played on the weekend? When it comes to rock 'n roll, Lonnie Baby, you're a man after my own heart.'

'No worries, Les,' beamed Lonnie. 'I'll burn them at the bar. And you'll get them in the mail by the end of the week. Along with the photos. I promise.'

Les raised his mug of coffee. 'Thanks, Lonnie,' he smiled. 'Maybe you're not such a bad bloke after all.'

THE END

Les Norton and the Case of the Talking Pie Crust

ROBERT G. BARRETT

Les is quite happy resting up after the flu, when Warren has to tip him into an earn. Norton's mate from the Albanian Mafia, Bodene Menjou, is planning to make the most politically correct movie ever made in Australia, *Gone With the Willy Willy*, and has a script stolen. If Les can find it, a lazy $50,000 could fall in. How can Norton say no?

After almost getting his head blown off in a drug lab, being attacked by crazed women with broomsticks, and beaten up by monstrous drag queens, Les is wondering if it is all worth it. The trip to Terrigal and the magical mystery tour with Marla is good. And Topaz with her chicken soup is an unexpected delight. But apart from that, Les doesn't find much joy at all in his search for the missing film script. Especially not trapped in a fight for his life with a sadistic giant, where only one thing can save him: the Mongolian Death Lock.

Set in Bondi and Terrigal, Robert G. Barrett's latest Les Norton adventure, *The Case of the Talking Pie Crust*, is vintage Les Norton doing exactly what he does best: his worst. And proves once again why Robert G. Barrett is, according to *The Australian*, the king of popular fiction.

'Barrett weaves a cracking tale' *Herald Sun*

Tesla Legacy

ROBERT G. BARRETT

'Forget the bloody Da Vinci Code, Mick. We've got to crack the Tesla Legacy. If we don't, we're both dead.'

Newcastle electrician Mick Vincent had almost everything in life he wanted. Jesse Osbourne, the Stockton bookshop owner he loved. A big house at Bar Beach. Not to mention a 1936 Buick Roadmaster ... in fact, the only thing Mick was missing was a pressure plate for his cherished car. Through a strange old lady, Mick finds his pressure plate. He also finds a diary belonging to Nikola Tesla, the electronics genius reputed to be smarter than Einstein. But just what did Tesla build in outback New South Wales in 1925?

The Pentagon knows, and the race is on to be the first to find the Tesla Legacy. Mick and Jesse's only clues are a lost mountain of copper ore and an old racehorse called Tears of Fire.

Robert G. Barrett's novel The Tesla Legacy, set in Newcastle, Muswellbrook, Scone and mysterious Burning Mountain in New South Wales, is an action-packed, pace-driven thriller woven with intrigue and a delightful touch of humour and romance, and an ending guaranteed to send chills down your spine. Proving once again why author Robert G. Barrett is, according to the Australian newspaper, the king of popular fiction.

> 'Do not read this book in public unless you are
> comfortable laughing in front of strangers'
> *Sydney Morning Herald*
> 'a cracker of a read ... a good touch of the smarts and
> lashings of heartfelt humour' *West Australian*
> 'a flat-out terrific yarn' *The Australian*

Crime Scene Cessnock

ROBERT G. BARRETT

Les is back and on the detox …

All it took was a summer's day and a flat tyre on his push-bike, and Les is out on bail and on the run from a gun-happy street gang intent on a drive-by. So, with Warren's help, Les Norton defendant, becomes Len Gordon film director, safely ensconced at the ultra-swish Opal Springs Health Resort till Eddie can sort things out back in Sydney.

Unfortunately, the first thing Les finds on arrival is motivational guru Alexander Holden dead at the front gate. Then, before you can say 'soya beans with tahini and lime dressing', the cops arrive and Les is up to his neck in a land of a thousand acronyms, fighting off steroid-happy body builders, sex-crazed socialites, violent greyhound owners - and, worst of all, caffeine withdrawals - while at the same time matching wits with the four acrimonious writers-in-residence. Was Alexander Holden murdered? Or was it an accident? Find out in the gripping climax and food fight when all is revealed – in the library.

Robert G. Barrett's latest Les Norton adventure, *Crime Scene Cessnock*, set in New South Wales's beautiful Pokolbin Valley, is a whodunnit with a difference, and proves once again why Barrett is, to quote *The Australian* newspaper, 'the king of popular fiction'.